Greyladies

MURDER AT THE FLOOD

Born in 1915 in Wallasey, Cheshire, Mabel Esther Allan knew by the age of eight that she was going to be a writer. Poor eyesight blighted her schooldays, but she enjoyed ballet and folk dancing, being inspired to some degree by Elsie J. Oxenham's Abbey series, and she later taught classes for the English Folk Dance Society. Her first book, *The Glen Castle Mystery,* was accepted in 1939 but publication was delayed until after the war. Her own war work included the Women's Land Army, prep school teaching and being Nursery Warden in a factory in the Liverpool slums. After the war she travelled widely, especially liking Paris, New York, Wales and Scotland, and a sense of place became an important part of her fiction.

As well as writing under her own name, she used the pseudonyms Jean Estoril, Anne Pilgrim and Priscilla Hagon. She was a prolific children's author, but her only published novel for adults was *Murder at the Flood.*

MURDER AT THE FLOOD

MABEL ESTHER ALLAN

Greyladies

Published by
Greyladies
an imprint of The Old Children's Bookshelf
175 Canongate, Edinburgh EH8 8BN

© The Estate of Mabel Esther Allan

Originally published by Stanley Paul, 1957
This edition first published 2009
Design and layout © Shirley Neilson 2009

ISBN 978-0-9559413-9-9

All rights reserved. No part of this publication may be
reproduced, stored in or introduced into a retrieval system, or
transmitted, in any form or by any means (electronic,
mechanical, photocopying, recording or otherwise) without the
prior written permission of the above copyright owners and the
above publisher of this book.

Set in Sylfaen / Perpetua
Printed in Great Britain by the MPG Books Group.
Bodmin and King's Lynn

MURDER AT THE FLOOD

Chapter 1
A WIND FROM THE NORTH

THE wind came howling from the north across the vast grey-green stretch of the marsh. It had blown all day, menacingly, working Emily Varney up into an ever-increasing state of tension and vague foreboding. Normally she loved the spreading marsh, the distant sea and the long channels of water in which red and blue boats rested, but something about the dead grey sky that had hung over the village of Marshton all day, and some quality in that bitterly cold, tireless wind, filled her with a nameless fear. She had kept the feeling under control during the early part of the day, for usually she was a reasonably well-balanced person, not given to premonitions or needless uneasiness, but now, alone in the solid brick and flint Vicarage on its slight eminence above the red-roofed village, she was suddenly forced to abandon all pretence of work and to wander restlessly about the darkening house.

It was not much more than six o'clock on a day early in March, but already all colour had gone from the scene that lay before her as she stood at the landing window. Even the bright pantiles of the roofs below had almost merged into the greyness. She could see the white strip of the coast road snaking along beside the marsh, straddled by the small, familiar village, and in the distance the great mill at Blane-next-the-Sea was black against the sky. The wind shook the pane as she stood there and the empty house was filled with its long scream.

Mrs. Sainty, the cook-housekeeper, had gone into Norwich in the early afternoon, as she generally did on her half-day, and would probably not be back till late, but Richard should have returned some time ago. He had only gone to make two or three calls on sick parishioners, calls that she had begged him not to make at all, for he had a bad cold and should not be out in the bitter wind.

Standing there on the shadowy landing, slim and tall against the heavy sky, Emily Varney was conscious of the aching need for her husband that filled her sometimes, a need that was not always satisfied when he was with her. It was a need that would have amazed the villagers could they have known about it, for the popular opinion was that Mrs. Varney was rather hard; altogether too smart and good-looking for a parson's wife.

But the truth was that Emily Varney loved her husband passionately, as passionately as she had ever done at their marriage two years before. She knew that he loved her in return, but she knew—or suspected—that there were depths in him that she had never so far reached. His was a controlled nature and at times he was woundingly remote. And the remoteness had increased just lately. She knew that something was worrying him and she strongly suspected that a letter he had received that morning belonged to the same problem. After reading it he had crumpled it up with unusual violence and had thrust it into his pocket.

She had known soon after they met, when he had been Vicar of the village of Melverley near her own home, that he was, strangely perhaps, the only man for her. Her friends and acquaintances had raised their eyebrows, and some had gone so far as to express their surprise when the engagement was announced. Emily was twenty-eight then, highly successful and very nearly beautiful. Richard Varney was ten years older, a bachelor, and it was said of him that at some time he had had an unfortunate love affair, which had left him a trifle soured. Emily had not thought him soured at all; then his slight remoteness had been an added attraction, and they had much in common in their shared love of books, music and the Norfolk countryside.

They had married and soon afterwards had come to live at Marshton, and somehow Emily had kept the secret of her success from the villagers, feeling, quite rightly, that they would not think it suitable that the Vicar's wife should be the well-known writer of somewhat scholarly detective fiction. Her books were published under the name of A. E. Sebastian and, until recently, no one at all had even realized that there was a secret. Mrs. Sainty knew all about the books, of course, for she had been in service with Emily's mother for many years, but she was a taciturn creature who found no difficulty in keeping things to herself. She had never read a word of any of the books, having a passion—rather surprising in one so gaunt and practical—for light romantic literature.

There was one person at least in the village who would have been interested to know that A. E. Sebastian and Emily Varney were one and the same, and that was Mr. Valentine Pike, a retired business man from Norwich, who was an inveterate reader of detective fiction, from the highest to the lowest form of it. But Emily certainly had no wish for him to know. She did not care for Mr. Pike, who was loud-voiced, decidedly inquisitive and interfering. He called these last two characteristics "taking an interest in his fellow men", and he was popular enough in the Roaring Bull down on the marsh road, but life would definitely not be so easy once he knew.

Her considerable fan-mail was sent on from her publishers in large, plain envelopes, and her study was upstairs in a part of the house to which no caller ever penetrated. It was therefore all the more incomprehensible how the information had leaked out—and to Thomas Long of all people! How could he have learned the fact, since he had not the slightest connection with the writing world? Still, it was said of him that he had an uncanny way of ferreting out people's secrets—the things that they thought no one could know.

Emily thought of Thomas Long with a shudder; less because he felt he had some hold over her than because she suspected that there were others in the village who were in a far worse position. She had no real knowledge; it was instinct, slightly helped by the gossip that she could not fail to hear, however firmly she discouraged it.

Well, let Thomas Long do his worst and tell the whole of Marshton that she was a famous writer! It could do no great harm, really, beyond occasioning greater speculation as to why she had married Richard. She could hear the wagging tongues speculating on the money she must make. Well, let them talk! Richard would not mind. He respected her work and there was no jealousy or meanness in him. It was not her work or her money that caused the slight shadow between them. It was something in Richard's past that he had never been able to tell her, though sometimes she had thought him on the point of it.

Anyway, she had taken no notice of Thomas Long's bald but not ill-written letter. Letter . . . She remembered again the one that Richard had seemed to hate so much that morning. But Thomas Long could have nothing on Richard—that was letting her mind wander too far.

At the window Emily stirred restlessly. Why was the wind having this effect on her? She never enjoyed the gales that came from the north, but they had never really bothered her before. There were galley proofs awaiting her downstairs, proofs on which she had done a considerable amount of work since half-past three, but they would have to wait. Her powers of concentration had gone and even Mr. Merrow's urgency could not drive her back to work.

Her publisher had never visited her before, but that morning he had driven over from Norwich, where he happened to be staying. He had had lunch with herself and Richard and afterwards the pair of them had got down to business, for her own trips to London were few and far between and there was much to discuss. He had left the proofs with her, urging haste, for the book was to appear as soon as possible, and Emily, a quick worker, had already made good progress. But the wind had certainly put an end to any further work; the wind and Richard's continued absence.

Running her hand through her silky dark hair, she turned from the window and moved to another one that looked across the wintry garden to the rough lane that went quickly down from the church to the village, passing the Vicarage gate and plunging out on to the marsh road between the general shop and the little brick and flint school building.

There was a figure coming down the lane from the churchyard, a young woman, who, even between the sheltering walls, was having to fight against the gale. It was quite light enough to recognize Caroline High, the schoolteacher, and light enough, too, to see that all was not well with her. As Emily watched, wanting only to see the tall figure of her husband, Caroline leaned for a moment against the far wall and buried her face in her hands. There was something about the tense, distressed figure that added to the lurking menace of the evening. What could be the matter with her, standing there as though she were fighting with nausea or deep distress? And would Emily receive any thanks if she went out and tried to discover if there was anything she could do?

Probably not, she thought wryly, for Caroline had never shown much desire to be friends with the Vicar's wife, nor with anyone else for the matter of that. She was a good teacher, efficient and kindly enough with the somewhat stolid and unimaginative children of the marsh village, but she made no secret of her dislike of her own native county and no one expected her to stay very long in Marshton now that her mother was dead. Emily imagined rather than saw, as the girl's hands fell away from her face and she went on slowly and with strange unsteadiness down the lane, the straight, tight line of the red lips that should have been full and alive, and the secret green eyes that gave beauty to the interesting but unnaturally tense face.

"I ought to go after her!" Emily said aloud, but already the girl had disappeared behind a higher wall lower down the lane.

Emily liked Caroline and would have been glad to be friends with someone intelligent and young, but there was a grimness about the younger woman, a hardness that made even the beginnings of friendship impossible. That Caroline was deeply unhappy Emily knew, though why it was not easy to see, unless perhaps it was merely that she missed her mother and was unloved. But no, it was more than that. The shadow had lain on Caroline High when she had come home from London a year ago to nurse her mother and teach in the village school.

And still there was no sign of Richard! Shivering with cold, for there were draughts on the landing and the bitter wind seemed to penetrate into her bones, Emily went downstairs again and into the sitting-room, where a roaring fire shed brilliant, flickering light. She drew the curtains to hide the dismal garden, and, switching on the light, made a movement to turn on the radio. But at that moment there was a loud knock at the front door.

Not Richard, surely? For Richard had his key. And not Stephan, her nephew, either, for Stephan also had a key and would be only too glad to use it to get in out of the wind, in spite of the fact that he had braved it to go for one of his long tramps that afternoon.

When Emily opened the door, letting in a wandering gust of icy wind, though the porch faced south-east, a child stood on the doorstep, straight fair hair blowing round a white, cold face.

"Betony! What on earth are you doing out in this wind? And it's growing dark, too!"

The child said nothing for a moment, then spoke with a rush in a voice that was softer and more rounded than might have been expected of Thomas Long's daughter. But it was from her mother that Betony got her voice and her clearly etched, sensitive face.

"Oh, Mrs. Varney, p-please may I b-borrow the Yeats again? The poems are so lovely, and I d-did copy some, but not all the ones I wanted. And I've been trying to remember the one that starts 'The host is riding from Knocknarea . . .' I'll t-take the greatest care of it if—"

"Good gracious, child!" Emily drew her into the hall and shut the door. Switching on the hall light she realized what she had suspected before, that Betony was half-dead with cold. Her face was blue, not white, and her almost colourless lips quivered to show her uneven but attractive little teeth.

Betony Long was twelve, inclined to be small for her age but wiry. Her face was much too aware for so young a girl and far too marked by suffering, but she could be gay at times and she had a mind that consciously and rather desperately sought after beauty. She and Emily had been friends for some time, since the day the previous summer when Emily had come upon her far out on the marsh, crouching amongst the dull purple sea lavender, reading poetry aloud to herself. Emily had sat down just above her in the dry, rustling grass and somehow a cautious intimacy had been born. Emily loved the marsh in summer, when the great sky arched overhead and the long channels of water were very blue, and Betony loved it, too, it seemed, passionately. She sought refuge there when her home became unbearable, as, in fact, it nearly always was.

Betony had never talked much about her father, but it was not necessary. Thomas Long had never been popular in the village, owing to a vicious tongue and his uncanny astuteness, but for the last year or so he had had bouts of heavy drinking, which resulted in a kind of increased malevolence towards everyone around him.

He kept a small garage on the marsh road, half a mile from his home, but was not a native of Marshton, and it was said that he came of much better circumstances. Certainly his wife had, but now she was little more than a pale, spiritless drudge, despised by her husband, who had wrought the change in her, and patently adored by Betony.

The child lived in hell, and it showed in her face and in her withdrawal into another, more satisfying world, but she was proud. She had not confided very greatly in Emily Varney, but she had grasped eagerly at the other's knowledge and kindness, had borrowed books and done her best to discuss them intelligently. She attended the High School in the nearest town, a fact that infuriated her father, who did not want a well-educated, critical daughter any more than he wanted a dispirited, quailing wife. But over that Marian Long *had* shown spirit. Betony was clever and should take the place she had won at the High School. So she had fought to provide her daughter with the necessary clothes and Betony adored school, though she did not make many friends.

Now Emily looked at her in some horror.

"Come into the sitting-room. There's a glorious fire there. But you ought not to be out on a night like this. Your mother..."

Betony followed her rather draggingly. The belt of her shabby navy blue raincoat was unfastened and hung down untidily and her fawn lisle stockings were twisted. As the child crouched over the fire Emily saw with a sense of shock that she still wore her satchel.

"Haven't you been home yet? Were you kept late at school?"

"No-o. I-I stayed. I was tidying the cupboards, and Miss Downe h-had to stay to mark some b-books so she didn't mind." Betony was still shivering and there was something in her eyes that Emily hated to see there.

"But you get off the bus at your own gate pretty well."

"I kn-know. But there was no one about and I w-wanted the Yeats, so I went up the track to the ch-churchyard." Betony gave something that was very like a shudder. "And then I c-came down here and..."

Emily whisked her galley proofs out of the way. It was unlikely that Betony would recognize them for what they were, but while there was still a chance that Thomas Long might not come out with her secret she might as well do her best to keep it. She had only brought her work downstairs because her study was getting the full force of the wind. She bent to one of the many bookcases and ran her long, white fingers over the familiar books until she found the thick one with the leather binding.

"Well, here are the poems. Would you like the plays as

well? Keep them for as long as you like. You ought to have a hot drink, but it's after half-past six and your mother will be worried. Besides, it's getting very dark. I should go down the lane to the village and up the main road."

For the main road cut down through the flat country inland, and half the houses of Marshton, including Betony's own home, were on it. The paths through the churchyard would be uninviting on this wild evening and the child looked haunted enough already.

On an impulse Emily suddenly asked:

"Why didn't you want to go home?"

Betony rose sharply from her crouching position and answered equally abruptly, this time almost without stammering:

"I couldn't face it, Mrs. Varney. Last night—it was awful! My father was very drunk and he hit my mother and said dreadful things to me. He said I was getting to be too much of a bloody lady and he'd not have a blasted little chit of twelve looking at him like that. Oh, and—and much worse than that. I—I can't *tell* you the things he said." Her face quivered.

It was difficult to know what to say and Emily regretted her question. She answered gently:

"It's a wretched situation and something ought to be done. Something will *have* to be done, Betony. But your mother needs you. I should hurry home as quickly as you can."

"Yes, Mrs. Varney. And thank you for the books. I think Yeats is perfect," said Betony earnestly. "I wish I could live in a little house on an island. Innisfree is a real place, isn't it?"

"It's in Lough Gill in County Sligo, but I believe its real name is Cat Island," said Emily, rather absently.

"I like even that." Betony made her way to the door. "I could keep some cats, couldn't I? A ginger one, and perhaps a grey one. We had a cat once, but father kicked it and mother had it put to sleep. But most of all I like 'The wind blows out of the gates of the day, The wind blows over the lonely of heart . . .' It's frightening, though. Do you hate the wind, Mrs. Varney?"

"I rather do tonight," said Emily. Then, in sudden compunction: "Betony, I'll come with you. I'm waiting for my husband and Stephan, but—"

But Betony did not seem to like the idea.

"No, thank you, Mrs. Varney. I'll run, and I'll go through the village. Thank you very, very much." And then she was speeding away down the path that wound between the bare flower-beds. At the gate she hesitated for a moment and the watching Emily caught her breath. Was it Richard at last? But it was a shorter, stockier figure, wearing a light tweed overcoat.

"Oh, damn and hell!" she said under her breath. She wanted no more visitors, for she felt that she could hardly talk coherently now. What on earth could John Abel-Otty *want?*

Mr. John Abel-Otty, writer of books about Norfolk topography and ornithology, was a great talker and was rather inclined to believe that everyone was anxious to listen to him at all times. He lived with his wife—a rather stiff, house-proud woman with little warmth—in an attractive small flint house down on the marsh, nearly opposite to the school, and was a fairly frequent visitor at the Vicarage.

"But I don't want him now!" Emily thought. "I shall tell him that I'm busy—anything! I hope that child gets home all right. I wish that Richard would come."

Mr. Abel-Otty advanced with his head down against the buffeting wind. When he reached the porch and his face became visible he was smiling. He looked, in fact, immensely pleased with himself.

"More so than usual," thought Emily uncharitably, though she really liked him well enough. He could be extremely interesting when one was in the right mood.

"Good evening, Mrs. Varney. Though really one can hardly call it good. I don't remember such a wind, though it's sheltered enough at the bottom of the lane."

There was nothing for it but to ask him in and Emily conducted him reluctantly to the sitting-room. He plumped himself down in an armchair near the fire and produced a pipe.

"Mind if I smoke? This is certainly a grand fire! Just what's needed on a night like this. I came up because I wondered if your husband—"

"I'm afraid he's out. I can't think where he's got to, as a matter of fact. I—"

"Oh, well, I can wait a few minutes, if you don't mind? I want to know if he'll lend me those old maps he has of the coast here. He did let me have them once before, if you remember. In fact, I'm hoping he'll allow me to have them reproduced in my latest book. You see . . ." And he was well launched on the subject of his new work. Emily strove to listen, but her ears were all the time straining to hear sounds above the wind.

When a key turned in the lock of the front door she was across the room in a moment, moving with the easy grace and speed that was one of her greatest attractions. But it was not Richard who seemed blown into the hall; it was Stephan, red-faced and cold-looking, bringing with him a feeling of unexpended energy.

"I thought you were Richard!" said Emily, making signs to show him that there was a visitor in the sitting-room.

Stephan heard the uneasiness and tension in her voice and looked at her in some surprise. He admired his aunt by marriage and had rarely known her to sound so agitated.

"No. Why, is he out? I thought he had a cold and it's a devil of a night. You can hear the sea thundering on the bank. Did you know that there's a flood warning on? They were saying in the pub that it's one of the highest tides of the year."

"Did you have a good walk?" Emily asked conventionally, as Stephan unwound his scarf and hung it and his overcoat on a peg in the hall. Flood warnings were no new thing and she had learned to take little notice of them.

"Oh, so so," said Stephan laconically. "About ten miles, I should say, and then I ended up at the Roaring Bull with Colonel Pashley and that ass Pike."

"Shhh! I've got Mr. Abel-Otty in there."

Stephan's look said, "What on earth does *he* want?" but he made no comment; merely strode into the room, and, with a casual nod to the visitor, stood astride the hearthrug. He was a big young man of twenty-five or so, not handsome really, but with a likeable, clear-cut face. Just now his whole manner expressed impatience, for Stephan Varney was finding life dull and he was by no means resigned to his fate as a partial invalid. He worked in London, having a good job in a shipping firm, and he was also passionately devoted to sport. He rode, he ski-ed when he had the chance, he played tennis like a professional and was no mean cricketer, and in winter he was a keen soccer player. It was during the latter game, nearly two and a half months before, that he had received the kick that had put him on his back for over a month with a detached retina in his left eye. The experience of lying immovable for so many weeks had shaken and sobered him and so had his weakness when he was at last allowed to go about again. But it was the embargo on all violent movement for some time, and on all games for two years, that had really cut him. The retina had gone back into place, and there was a good chance that the eye would be almost normal in future, but to Stephan Varney it was a constant fret that he could not bend down, could not travel on buses and must avoid all jerky movement. But being, on the whole, a good-tempered and surprisingly thoughtful person for one so full of energy he had striven to hide his frustration when he came to stay at Marshton Vicarage to recuperate. Once strong in himself he had taken many long walks, since they were the only exercise possible to him, and in a few days now he was returning to London and to work.

"They're not easy about the bank," he said conversationally after a moment. "But Colonel Pashley says it's held pretty well for hundreds of years and there's no real reason why it should be breached now."

"Yes, it held when there was that terrible flooding up the coast a few years ago. A fine piece of engineering!" said Mr. Abel-Otty, glad to be back on what was almost his present subject. "Built by Flemish workmen like others along the coast . . ."

Once more a key turned in the outer door and once more Emily sped towards the hall. This time it was her husband who stood there, his usually pale face red from the sting of the wind.

"Richard, I've been worried to death about you! Out in this awful wind . . ."

Richard Varney looked at her almost vaguely and then gave two explosive sneezes.

"Come in to the fire. You'll get pneumonia! *What's* the matter?" Emily knew then that the obscure feeling of impending disaster had not been imagination.

Her husband followed her into the sitting-room. He nodded absently, as though he scarcely saw them, to the other two men. He stood there, tall and tense, his greying hair unusually untidy.

"Thomas Long's lying in the churchyard. He's dead!"

Chapter 2
INOPPORTUNE MURDER

"DEAD?" said Emily stupidly, staring at him. She hardly knew what she had expected, but it was certainly not this. "In the *churchyard?*"

"Near the south porch, just by the Starlings' grave," said her husband, still in that almost absent or bemused voice.

"The *south* porch?" Emily found to her slight annoyance that she could not stop repeating his words. But there was reason for her astonishment. Thomas Long had never set foot in the church, and his only reason for being in the churchyard was surely to take the short cut from opposite his house, up the narrow track, across the north of the churchyard and down Church Lane, past the Vicarage, to the far side of the village. In winter, when the north and east winds blew so violently and coldly, the south door into the church was always the one that was open, but . . .

"He *can't* have been going into the church!" said Emily stupidly.

Stephan and Mr. Abel-Otty were staring in deepest interest, but Mr. Abel-Otty, at least, did not look surprised. "It's all that drink he's been taking," he said briskly. "I know he never seemed drunk in the usual way, but it's common knowledge that he was pouring it into himself. I suppose he had a stroke or a heart attack. He wasn't a young man. Over fifty and big. That type—"

"Then perhaps he isn't dead," said Stephan helpfully and quite cheerfully. "We'd better go up there and bring him down, and I suppose his wife had better be told. Not that she'll be very sorry, surely? Nor that poor, flaxen-haired kid."

"He's certainly dead," said Richard Varney, dropping suddenly into one of the deep armchairs and speaking with much greater decision. He was not normally a vague nor indecisive man. "There was no doubt about it, really, but I felt his pulse and it had stopped."

"Well, we'd better ring up the police," said Emily. "Rust will handle it for us; I don't see why we should be involved any more than necessary. Will you do it, Stephan? Richard's all in, and I'll make him some tea at once and put some rum into it." Suddenly she felt easier again and glad of action. Something that she recognized as relief was surging through her mind. Thomas Long dead! Why, it was the best possible thing that could have happened. The village would be a better place without him and her own somewhat paltry secret would be safe now.

She stood still for a moment, looking at her husband. The discovery had certainly upset him; he looked tired and old.

"I've been so worried to think of you out in that terrible wind. I thought—I wondered . . . Did you have any tea while you were out, Richard?"

Her husband looked at her vaguely again.

"Yes, I had some with old Mrs. Gotts. She insisted and I never *can* get away, poor old soul. And then I went up to the church. I went in through the vestry door and was there for about half an hour. Then I—I left by way of the south porch and I saw something dark amongst the graves. It was getting dusk—in fact the light was very bad—but still . . . Yes, we'll have to telephone to the police, but I doubt if Rust can handle it."

"Why not?" Stephan asked briskly. "He's quite efficient for a village policeman."

"Because," said his uncle, "Thomas Long has been murdered."

"Murdered?" Stephan and Mr. Abel-Otty spoke together, but Emily stood motionless and wordless.

"Yes, murdered. It can't possibly have been accident. He's lying on his face and the back of his skull has been cracked."

"Perhaps," said Mr. Abel-Otty, puffing great clouds of rather offensive tobacco smoke into the room, "he fell and cracked his head against a tombstone. Then rolled over on to his face."

"I hardly think so," said Richard Varney. "It struck me as being quite impossible. He may have been drunk and he may have fallen of his own accord, but someone else brought about his death. In fact, I found the stone."

"The stone?"

"Yes, it was lying close to him—a great piece of flint. There's plenty of it in the churchyard from that crumbling wall, but it wasn't too dark to see . . ." And Richard Varney suddenly looked so sick and white that Emily cried passionately:

"That horrible man! He's always caused trouble here and now he's going to cause some more. I don't wonder someone murdered him—if anyone did. And I almost hope they're never caught!"

"My dear!" Her husband made a cautionary gesture and

Emily caught herself up sharply. It was not like her to lose all control, to speak her mind almost hysterically.

"I wish it hadn't been you who had to find him," she said much more quietly. "And now ring up the police and I'll make the tea. The kettle has been on the boil for hours."

But as Richard Varney motioned Stephan away and bent forward to take up the receiver, and Emily herself moved towards the door, there was a thundering knock at the front door, followed by the sound of a voice calling shrilly and incoherently. The words were lost, however, in the noise of the wind.

"Someone else found the body!" said Stephan flippantly. He had had no love for Thomas Long and was hardly distressed by the news of his violent end.

But when the door was opened it was Mrs. Sainty who burst in, clutching a shabby umbrella, a bulging string bag and an equally bulging plastic handbag that had seen much better days.

"Oh! Oh!" she cried, her grey hair wild and her unbecoming hat hanging over one ear, held by the stout hatpin that she always wore. "Oh, how I got up here no one will ever know! Never should have done if this terrible wind hadn't been behind me! I got the earlier bus because there was nothing on at the pictures and of course I went right round to the shop. No churchyards for me once it's dark! And I heard it coming as I passed round the back of the bus. Like an express train—believe me! But we should be safe here and thank the good God for letting me get here safely. There's a many will be dead this very minute."

She collapsed, panting, against the banisters and Emily

seized her by one thin shoulder.

"What's coming, Mrs. Sainty?"

Mrs. Sainty raised a white face and her breath still came with difficulty.

"The water! The bank's gone and the water's coming! I heard it roaring nearer and nearer as I started up the lane and my legs just wouldn't carry me at first. I looked back and saw it hit Mr. Abel-Otty's house. Like a bomb, it was, and one wall just seemed to crumble. They'll be up here—all those who can. But they'd be caught in their houses—they'd never even know!"

In the sitting-room doorway she paused, leaning on Emily's arm, and her eyes took in the presence of the three men.

"You'll have to go to the rescue. Go and see what you can do, for God's sake! I'll put my kettles on and switch on the immerser. We'll have to air all the blankets. But just wait while I get my breath!"

Mr. Abel-Otty had risen, his stocky figure suddenly tense. Then he perceptibly relaxed.

"My wife! For a moment I thought she was at home, then I remembered that she's gone to have tea with Mrs. Pashley. But the Pashleys' house stands only a few feet higher than our own. If you'll excuse me I'll go at once." He knocked out his pipe, thrust it into his pocket and crossed the room rapidly.

"Tell everyone you see to come here or to the church," said Emily, gathering her wits. "I'll go and find blankets and hot-water bottles while you see to the supply of hot water, Mrs. Sainty. We'll need every kettle in the house."

"Let's go and have a look from the landing window first," said Stephan, and, though he could not run, had such a long stride that he was immediately ahead of his uncle and aunt. Mr. Abel-Otty hesitated and then followed them. It would do no harm to try to see the lie of the land, or rather the water, before he went plunging to the rescue.

"All my books!" he said, half to himself, as he climbed the stairs. "And my notes. Dear, dear me!"

The daylight was now almost gone, but there was just enough to make them all draw in their breath sharply. For where there had been miles of marshland there was now only a tossing, heaving sea. It broke not more than a hundred yards away at the foot of the hill that held Vicarage and church, and the little houses below looked like arks, half-submerged. Swiftly Emily moved to another window that gave a wide view westwards and inland. The water there was still moving, not perhaps as fast as an express train, but quickly enough to leave damage and death in its wake, giving only those people who had noticed what was happening time to quit their houses and farms and perhaps not even then.

For seconds only they took in the scene and then, with a muffled exclamation, Mr. Abel-Otty turned on his heel.

"I'll be off. Perhaps I can get hold of a boat. Are you coming?" to Stephan.

"He mustn't do anything rash," said Emily automatically, but Stephan merely snorted and strode down into the hall, dragging his overcoat off the peg as he passed.

"I must go, too," said Richard Varney, but, as Emily

opened her mouth to protest, Mr. Abel-Otty said over his shoulder as he wrenched at the front door:

"I shouldn't, Varney. You'll be needed here."

"Yes, I suppose so. I'll get the church ready." Richard Varney had recovered himself and spoke quickly. "The old and sick and the very young children can come here. The rest must go in the church and so must all the furniture and possessions that are rescued. I'll get up there and light the oil-stoves and the lamps, and I'll open the west door so that—"

"So that no one will see the body," Emily finished for him, on her knees by the deep cupboard on the landing. She threw out blankets in piles. "I'll come and join you in a very few minutes. Mrs. Sainty can cope here. She's got her head screwed on. Take the big electric lamp. You can put it on the church steps to show people the way, and do—do take care. You never had that tea and rum."

"Others will certainly need it more than I. What's a cold in the head?" asked her husband, as he plunged down the stairs. The front door opened and closed again.

It crossed Emily's mind that an incredible number of things can happen in a very few minutes. It was no time at all since Richard had come home at last and now he was gone again.

Frantically she threw out more blankets and two mattresses, rushed into the bedrooms and switched on electric fires, collected hot-water bottles from the bathroom. The actions occupied only a few further minutes, but all the time wild, disturbing thoughts shot through her mind.

The wind, apparently increasing in force; the flood; the

people trapped below in their homes, perhaps struggling in darkness and rising water; the body of Thomas Long lying in the churchyard.

Murder! Though she had written of it often, had turned over many a complicated and horrifying crime in her mind and had discussed many another with her father, who had been Chief Commissioner at Scotland Yard before his sudden death, it had never struck so near her before. Questions and pictures floated frighteningly before her eyes. Why did it have to be Richard who found the body? Anyone, anyone else! What had Thomas Long been *doing* so near the south porch? And who had been lurking there amongst the tombstones on such an impossible evening? The path to the north was fairly frequently used, but anyone who passed the church on the south side should logically have been intending to enter.

Suddenly she remembered Caroline High, so obviously distressed, perhaps nauseated. Had *she* perhaps seen the body? Could *she*—and Emily remembered a day, not so very long before, when she had come upon the schoolteacher and Mr. Thomas Long talking on the marsh road. Caroline was clutching her bicycle and had broken off the conversation abruptly as Emily approached, but it had been impossible not to note the raised voices and the distress and fright on Caroline's face. At the time, however, she had merely thought that Mr. Long must have made one of his unpleasant remarks and she had supposed that Caroline could deal with him. Perhaps she should have taken more notice of Caroline's expression and done something to help. Perhaps she should have forced her confidence on that occasion and this evening when she saw her in the lane.

"Minding one's own business might be carried too far," thought Emily. "But surely, surely she can't have had sufficient cause to use that flinty stone?"

No, it could not have been Caroline, who had such an air of fastidious withdrawal. She did not look capable of violence.

"But anyone—*anyone* can be violent if driven sufficiently," Emily thought, as she went hurriedly downstairs. "I might be myself. For Richard, certainly."

And another memory shot through her mind: Mrs. Sainty recounting to her a piece of village gossip, that Stephan had had a violent quarrel with Thomas Long near the garage. But Stephan himself had not mentioned it and he, of all people, could not have been in any way in Thomas Long's clutches. Stephan, she was ready to swear, had no secrets.

"Murder," thought Emily, as she hurried into the dining-room to put a light to the coal fire already laid in the grate, "is the very devil. It starts suspicions as soon as it happens. People might even suspect *me* if they knew of the letter. Or if Thomas Long had already hinted that he knew something about me. Maybe he'd done just that, because I ignored his letter. He wanted money, of course, but if he couldn't get that he was just the sort of man to enjoy revenge."

There were sounds outside; she heard them during a slight lull in the wind. Mrs. Sainty appeared in the kitchen passage as she wrenched at the fastening of the front door.

"I can cope here, if you want to be off to the church with your husband."

"I must go up, but I'll be back," Emily said over her shoulder. The wind burst into the hall with renewed fury and there were people on the path. In the forefront of the soaked, bedraggled and vociferous little band was old Mrs. Grief from the post office and general shop and her daughter, Minnie.

Minnie, a middle-aged spinster, lived up to her surname even more thoroughly than her mother, but just now there was ample reason for her bitterness and distress and Emily received them with warmth and gentleness, appalled at their story of escape. Minnie had heard the water coming because she had been "out at the back", and she had rushed her mother upstairs just in time. They had scarcely reached the upper story before the wall of water had broken round the stout little flint building.

"And all our stock floating up to the ceiling, let me tell you, and a dead dog brought in through the window when it broke!" Minnie's voice also broke, on a high wail.

They had been rescued almost at once by a boat hastily captured and rowed by Colonel Pashley, and with them were the Colonel's wife and Mrs. Abel-Otty, both cold, wet and bewildered.

"John told us to come up here. Said everyone was to come!" Mrs. Abel-Otty cried shrilly. "We met him at the foot of the lane—where the water comes to. He's got another boat, but with only one oar, and I begged him not to risk his life, but he wouldn't listen. Our house has gone, you know—one wall went straight away. And my best carpet in the sitting-room . . ." Her voice went off into a wail.

"An' all our day's takings! Do you be askin' someone to fetch 'em for us!" cried old Mrs. Grief. "I said to our Minnie—"

Her daughter rounded on her fiercely.

"Oh, shut up, ma! I couldn't get them. There wasn't time. And no one can get anything while the water's fifteen feet high, or more than that, likely enough." Indignation made her fretful voice suddenly brisk.

Desperately sorry for the party, but steeling herself to the certain knowledge that worse was to come, Emily installed them by the fire and left them to Mrs. Sainty's ministrations while she went upstairs with Mrs. Pashley to seek out all the dry clothes in the house. They would certainly be needed.

Mrs. Pashley, a sensible enough woman, though shaken by her experience and the terrifying but prompt rescue by boat, panted at her heels.

"Oh, my dear! I shall never forget it—never! There we were—Mrs. Abel-Otty and me—sitting gossiping by the fire. My husband had gone out for a stroll, though I told him he was crazy on such a night. However, it turned out a blessing that he *was* out and realized what was happening. The first we knew there was a sort of roar and water came pouring across the drawing-room floor. So we dashed upstairs just as the lights went out and the water was nearly up to the bedroom window when Henry came with the boat and Mrs. Abel-Otty nearly in hysterics about her carpet, though I told her it was no time to be thinking of carpets, new or old.

"And the little we saw as Henry rowed us to high ground

—it was terrible! People trapped everywhere and shouting their heads off, but you could hardly hear in the wind, and bodies floating by. And those lovely Friesian cows from Marsh Farm swimming for their lives and several dead already. There'll be nothing left of Marshton! I'm afraid it's the end of the village and of half the people in it. But there! I'm as bad as Mrs. Abel-Otty and this is no time for moaning and wailing. I'll leave that to Mrs. Grief, poor old soul. I must say she couldn't have chosen a better name! Yes, I'll go down and help Mrs. Sainty once I've got my wet clothes off. I'd better do that because my rheumatism's been bad this winter, as you know. You get off to the church, my dear. A woman will be wanted there and they'll be going up there from the main road."

Emily put on a winter coat, tied a scarf over her hair, and, taking a strong torch, set off across the garden to the lane. At the gate she met another party, even more incoherent than the first one. Some people were dragging pieces of furniture and others clutched bundles of bedding and clothing. A small boy held a shivering, whining dog in his arms, and another child, crying bitterly, clutched a terrified, soaking-wet cat.

Emily said a few words of comfort, though her voice seemed entirely blown away, and motioned them to go to the house. Some of them would have to camp out in the church later, as the very aged and sick were rescued, but just then warmth and hot drinks were the direst necessities.

She plunged off up the lane, which was almost quite dark now. The wind screamed over her head and somewhere behind her something fell with a crash. One of the

Vicarage chimney-pots, perhaps. Mostly she kept her head down, but when she reached the small iron gate that led into the churchyard she looked up. There was light behind the beautiful, plain windows in the north aisle of the church and she could see the tall, flint tower against the wild sky. Marshton Church was one of the finest buildings in that area of wonderful churches, high and light and with perfect proportions, though it was growing shabbier and more in need of repair with the passing of each year.

Stumbling a little, Emily used her torch to show her the path that went round to the west door. Once round the angle of the church a blaze of light shone out from the electric lamp on the steps, but there was no one in sight. She turned the heavy wrought-iron handle and pushed the great door, the same door that had admitted people to the church for many hundreds of years. At once she smelt the familiar odour of damp and oil-lamps and for a brief moment her eyes took in the scene. The lamps in the nave and chancel were alight and their glow fell dimly on the rounded Norman arches of the south aisle and on the more delicate Early English one above the chancel.

But it was only for a second that Emily was conscious, as always, of the beauty of the church. As the door shut with a clang behind her she looked round for Richard, seeking for his tall, black-clad figure in the midst of the bewildered and motley crowd that lingered on the old, faded Dutch tiles. The church was so big that the ancient pews, still with strangely carved bench-ends, only filled two-thirds of the centre aisle. At the west end of the nave there was a great stretch of the blue tiles, on which stood only the

Norman font with its weird animal carvings, and clustered round the font, some of them sitting on its steps and others crouching over the inadequate heating of the half dozen oil-stoves that were kept to warm the church in winter, were other survivors of the flood, including Mr. Valentine Pike, who seemed to have put himself in charge, for he was talking in rather a loud, commanding voice.

They all swung round to stare at Emily and she asked at once:

"Where's my husband?"

"In the vestry, bringing out two more stoves," said Mr. Pike briskly. "Mr. Herring here says he can mend them and we'll need all the heating we can get. I'll be off again, then. I've got a boat moored down the hill. Sheer luck that I managed to get hold of it. It was floating away up the main road and I plunged in and grabbed it. Nothing like having a boat on a night like this! Bad business. Don't see how we're to get everyone out." And he saluted Emily and went off, quite obviously rather pleased with himself for his efficiency.

"And he has every right to be," Emily told herself, as she spoke what words of comfort and encouragement she could. She arranged for one or two of the younger and more vigorous people to go down to the Vicarage for clothes and blankets, jugs of tea and anything else that would be useful, and then hurried off down the aisle to find her husband. Richard was just emerging from the vestry, his clothes very dusty, the rusty oil-stoves held in either hand.

"Oh, Richard, are you all right? Things are getting

organized, I think, but—"

"They'll need to be. We haven't really started yet," Richard Varney said grimly. "How cold this place is! How on earth are we going to heat it adequately? If we could get enough wood I suppose we might make a fire in the nave, but then we'd be smoked out."

"Richard, the body—?"

"Still there. No one knows and I hope they won't for a while," he assured her. "Even murder must take a back seat on an occasion like this, though I'd feel happier if we could get him indoors. I'll get Love to look at him when he comes up. But he's somewhere down in the village doing what he can, I'm told."

"I suppose he ought to see him as soon as possible," Emily said. She liked and trusted Dr. Love.

"So he ought. The fellow can't have been dead long when I found him."

Emily clutched at his hand, glad that he had put the stoves down. It was shadowy at the eastern end of the church and they were hidden behind a pillar.

"Richard, I've lost my nerve, I think. I'm being a fool. It was that awful wind and wondering where you were. I wish the wind would *stop!*" For the gale blew violently round the church, high on the hill above the flooded marsh.

Richard Varney was suddenly entirely with her and his voice was warm and reassuring.

"My dear, it's all right. About the murder, I mean. *I* didn't bump him off. That, I believe, is all you care about."

"Yes, it is, I suppose." Emily's voice shook a trifle. "But,

Richard, I didn't think—I didn't mean that *you*—"

"Of course you didn't. But other people may. I was up here alone from at least six till after half-past and I never heard a sound—couldn't, I suppose, because of the wind."

Then suddenly, for far too brief but how comforting a moment, he held her in his arms and their lips met. Her heart leaped and her body quivered with instant delight as she recognized his hunger, but a cold voice said in her mind:

"This is no time for any kind of happiness."

Almost at once he let her go and picked up the oil-stoves.

"We must get to work. But you looked so lost, Emily. We've got to make these people as comfortable as possible. Mrs. Herring and those two small children"—at that moment their wails filled the church—"must go down to the house. I think I hear some new arrivals."

"At least," thought Emily, following him, "he *is* near. He's never kissed me in the church before. I can cope with anything now."

The west door had opened again and an icy draught sighed down the nave. There was the sound of shrill, agitated voices and the thud of articles of furniture and suitcases being dumped down. Someone said loudly and tearfully:

"Do you be goin' back, Mr. Pike, sir, will you look for our Tibby? Out in the garden, he was, taking his evening stroll, when the water—"

"Oh, dear!" said Emily, catching up with her husband. "But Tibby'll climb up on a roof or something. It's awful, but there'll be worse than cats."

"Far worse," said the Vicar gravely, and continued to stride up the aisle, with the two old stoves clanking in his red, cold hands.

As Emily followed him the door opened again and Mrs. Long came in. She was white-faced, wild-eyed and soaking wet and she cried loudly:

"Has anyone seen my husband? He never came home for his tea, and I went down to the pub at six and he wasn't there. The garage was closed, because I went to see."

Everyone shook their heads, except for an old man who said:

" 'E was down at the pub when it opened at 'alf-past five an' drunk enough then, Missus. Reckon they didn't want to tell you 'e'd been and gone. 'E must keep that stuff in 'is petrol pumps."

There was a feeble laugh, hastily stifled as Mrs. Long looked round with a desperate, almost insane look.

"And what's the matter with Betony, I'd like to know? She won't come! I can't think what's got into the child. Mr. Pike rescued us from the bedroom window and said we were to come to the church, but Betony—Mrs. Love said she'd bring her. She's screaming down there at the foot of the hill."

The door opened once more and Mr. Pike and the doctor's pretty, pleasant-faced wife stood there, with Betony Long between them. The child looked so ill that Emily was startled and went forward quickly.

"Well, Betony dear? It's terrible, isn't it? But you're quite safe now, and the water will go down—"

"I won't stop here! I won't! I won't!" The child's voice

was high and unnatural and her face was dead-white, all the more startling under the smooth, very flaxen hair.

"Betony, stop it at once!" said her mother, taking some hold on herself.

Abruptly Betony was silenced. She gave a convulsive gulp and looked round dazedly. Then, apparently reassured by the homely sight of glowing stoves and scattered household effects, she said suddenly in quite a different tone:

"Oh, Mrs. Varney, I couldn't save the plays. They were on the sitting-room table. What *will* you say? But I've got the poems safely. I'd just taken them upstairs to my bedroom when the water came." And she disclosed the stout leather volume that she had been holding under her faded and darned navy blue cardigan.

"Never mind the plays," said Emily, torn with pity for her and wondering how long the greater horror could be kept from her. Betony had been afraid of her father, but the news of his violent death would sicken her, surely? Relief might come later. "I'll buy you a copy of the plays just as soon as the water goes down and we can get to a good bookshop. And now, Betony, I want you to help me. You'll do that, won't you?"

Betony looked at her mother and then nodded tremulously.

"Yes, Mrs. Varney. Of course I'll help. But—but—I—"

"She's such a highly strung child and the water and the darkness frightened her," said Mrs. Long suddenly, apparently quite steady.

"There was a dog!" said Betony, shuddering again. "It was dead and it bumped against the boat—"

Emily's voice rose clear and cool.

"Betony, could you amuse some of the smaller children while we get things organized? They're going to be taken to the Vicarage just as soon as we can arrange it, but meanwhile . . ."

Betony nodded again and went off across the old, worn tiles, walking sturdily in her strong school shoes. When she beckoned some of the little ones towards the Children's Corner they went to her after only the slightest hesitation. Most people, young and old, liked Betony Long.

Blankets and hot-water bottles were arriving in quantities from the Vicarage now, and more and more people poured into the church, all with tales of horror and distress to tell. Emily was suddenly relieved to see Stephan there with Colonel Pashley and Mr. Abel-Otty and snatched a brief word with him.

"Stephan, *do* remember that you're an invalid. I know it's maddening, but you *mustn't* carry things or row or anything."

Stephan pulled a rueful face.

"I haven't. I've been giving orders mainly. It's about all I'm good for."

"Well, someone has to. There are plenty of strong men in the village to get on with the rescue work. Why not go and help Richard to see that all the furniture goes at the top of the south aisle, and do get someone to tie that dog up. It'll bite someone in a minute."

Emily herself now seemed to be in several places at once. There was no time for thinking, only doing, comforting, occasionally exhorting, for some of the older children, worked up by the unusual circumstances, were growing troublesome.

Under Betony's direction the little ones were quietly and rather waveringly singing nursery rhymes in the Children's Corner. Their voices rose oddly above the din:

> "Baa, baa, black sheep,
> Have you any *wool*—?"

Suddenly the west door burst open and Dr. Love's eleven-year-old son, Peter, stood there. Emily had not known that he was out. The last time she had seen him he had been dragging up hassocks for people to squat on near the stoves. As he stood there, his face flaming with excitement, there was a sudden, odd hush. Even the wind died down.

"I say!" said Peter Love, clearly and with relish. "There's a body not far from the south door! I went out to—well, I had to go out, and I had my torch, so I went round out of the wind. I'm afraid it's Mr. Long and he's had no end of a bash on the head. He's stone cold and as dead as anything and I think my father ought to see him at once."

Chapter 3
NO COMMUNICATIONS

THE silence intensified at once.

"Just fancy!" said Peter Love. "A flood *and* a murder! It must be a murder, mustn't it? Because he's lying on his *face* and the back of his head—"

There was a sudden, heart-lifting scream and Mrs. Long fell in a heap on the tiles, narrowly missing one of the stoves.

Peter suddenly went rather white, as though realizing for the first time exactly what had happened and what he had said. He held something in his hand besides his torch; something small and silver. A pencil.

" 'C. High'," read Peter, in rather a bemused voice, staring at it.

"Where did you get that pencil?" asked Emily sharply, reaching his side before anyone. Attention was temporarily diverted from Mrs. Long.

"It was by the—the b-body," said Peter, proving by the increasing greenness of his face that he was not so hardened after all.

"There's another goin' to faint!" cried old Mrs. Gotts shrilly, from her place in the back pew, where she was twisting round to watch events. She had flatly refused to be taken down to the Vicarage, saying—with how great a justification she could not have known—that she wanted to see what was going on.

Until then Emily had not even known that Caroline High

was there, but now she saw her amongst the crowd near the piled furniture. She was swaying, and Stephen, who was nearest, put out his arm and seized her as she crumpled up. She collapsed against his chest, her untidy, dark red hair spreading across his green pullover.

At once the tension broke and pandemonium was let loose.

"Give them air!"

"Lay them flat! Has anyone got any brandy?"

"A body by the south porch. Thomas Long . . . Must have been drunk and hit his head against a stone!"

"Give them *air!* Someone clear a pew—"

"—Must have been a shock for the poor woman, even if she hated his guts. She looks like death herself!"

Eager hands lifted Mrs. Long and laid her in one of the pews and someone attempted to remove Caroline from Stephan's arms. He said harshly:

"She's all right. She's coming round. She just wants a chair."

Someone provided one and Caroline sat down shakily, her face ghastly. She was already wearing clothes that did not belong to her and they hung on her slim, tense body.

Suddenly Betony streaked across the nave, pushing her way between people. Behind her the smaller children began to wail, frightened by the commotion.

"Mother! Mother! Don't die! Mother!"

"It's all right. She isn't dead. Fetch some water for the child as well."

Betony crouched beside her mother, murmuring words that sounded like disconnected endearments, and presently

Mrs. Long raised her head. She accepted a cup of water in a work-worn but still delicately shaped hand.

"Is my husband really dead? Is the boy right? It gave me a shock, but I'm all right now."

"I don't want to see him!" Betony's voice rose to a wail.

"It's all right, dear. You shan't see him—"

"Good riddance to bad rubbish, *I* say!" said old Mrs. Gotts over the top of her pew, her wrinkled face avid with curiosity and some pity. She hadn't had such an exciting evening for ten years and it seemed to have improved her feeble condition. "But the lad said murder. Do 'e be right we shall—"

"Keep quiet, everybody!" That was Mr. Pike. "Don't let's have a panic. We've got trouble enough. Now then, Peter, my boy, before the Colonel and I go and investigate this— this matter, tell us exactly what you did see. Are you sure you aren't imagining it? Perhaps Mr. Long's just fallen—"

Peter Love was now sitting on the steps of the font, receiving his share of the water. The colour had come back into his face and he spoke clearly and with renewed assurance.

"He really is dead, sir. I looked at his head and then I *felt* him."

Emily Varney's eyes sought those of her husband. The scene had taken on all the elements of a particularly lurid nightmare.

Richard Varney strode forward suddenly, decisive and very calm.

"I think perhaps I'd better say a few words, though I had hoped to keep the matter from everyone for a while. I discovered the body soon after half-past six—at six-thirty-nine, to be precise—when I was leaving the church. It was then just light enough to see and I came to the same conclusion as Peter here, though with rather more cause. I knew at once that Thomas Long had been murdered. He could not possibly have hit his head, and, as a matter of fact, the stone that was used was lying beside him. To the best of my knowledge it's still there and I suggest that we touch nothing until Dr. Love has examined the body. I went straight down to the Vicarage and was just about to telephone to the police when Mrs. Sainty arrived with the news of the flood."

He paused, looking calmly round at the attentive faces.

"Let me beg of everyone to remain calm and it would be better if as few people as possible leave the church just now. When Dr. Love has seen the body we will take it round to the vestry. Mr. Abel-Otty is also aware of what happened, for he was at the Vicarage when I arrived home. Mr. Abel-Otty, perhaps—" And he turned to the other man, who had reached the church not long before.

But Mr. Pike had no intention of allowing anyone else to take charge on such an occasion. All his years of reading murder stories had been justified. Here was a murder almost on his very doorstep.

"With your leave," he said quickly, not caring in the least that he interrupted the Vicar, "I'll keep guard over the body until the doctor comes. It should have been done from the first, of course, but with all the excitement . . . And does anyone know where Rust is? He should be informed, I suppose, though I hardly think . . ." And his look implied that he defied any village policeman to deal with murder.

"Didn't you know?" asked Stephan, with barely concealed dislike. He hated to hand further power into Mr. Pike's hands. "He's at the Vicarage with a suspected fracture—leg. And he was trapped in icy water for half an hour into the bargain."

"Then we'll have to get in touch with the nearest police station as soon as we can," said Mr. Pike, regretfully. He would have liked to wipe out the whole police force as neatly as Rust had been disposed of, for he would surely never have the same chance again to dabble in real-life detection. "But meanwhile we must do our best to behave wisely. I'll go and take up my position, and, Pashley, perhaps you'll try to get hold of Dr. Love?"

They departed together and once more pandemonium broke out.

"But the silver pencil? Miss High's pencil!" a woman cried shrilly. "Do it be lyin' by the body it means—"

"I lost it!" said Caroline High, on a note of hysteria. "I didn't know where it was. I—"

"Can't you take her down to the other end and talk quietly to her?" Emily said imploringly to Stephan. "I know you don't like her, but . . ." Only that morning Stephan had remarked what a sour-looking girl she was and had said he liked his women cheerful.

Stephan hesitated.

"Oh, Lor'! What a thing to land me with! Why can't I be doing a man's job down in the village? For two pins—"

"No, you wouldn't," said Emily crisply. She understood

her nephew by marriage well enough. "You're not going to jeopardize everything by rowing and plunging about when there are fifty or more able-bodied men to do it. Surely you can feel some pity for the girl, Stephan? She needs someone intelligent and—"

"O.K. She certainly needs to get away from these harpies. I'll guard her for you."

When he made the suggestion Caroline looked at him dully, but made no protest. They went off down the nave and disappeared into the shadows of one of the side chapels.

Emily was conscious that she had a headache and she would have given a great deal to get away from the noise and increasing smells of the church. Certainly it was a very long time since the building had seen so much life. Briefly she thought of it as it had looked the previous afternoon when she had been there alone, arranging masses of daffodils and narcissi on the altar. Faint sunlight had poured in through the white and clear blue windows of the south aisle, lighting up the shabby, cream-washed walls and drawing dim colour from the old tiles. The wind had been blowing across the marsh, but not with frightening strength, and through one of the plain windows to the north she had suddenly seen the bright boats and the brighter roofs. And now—death and disaster and problems that had their humorous side, or would have, perhaps, when the flood was only a memory. Sanitary arrangements, for one thing. Something would have to be done about those quickly. She looked at old Mrs. Gotts and wondered what on earth was to be done about her. She was unable to walk a yard.

"We've got to get her down to the Vicarage," she thought, and went to find Richard.

"A row of buckets," said her husband briskly. "I've thought of it already, and some screens. There are those old ones in our attics. I've sent some of the men to fetch them and I didn't forget to ask them to bring disinfectant."

"But people like old Mrs. Gotts?"

"Heaven only knows," said her husband. "But people won't jib at a little thing like that. Won't have to. She'll never go down to the Vicarage while there's anything to see. Can you persuade the mothers to get some of the children ready to go there? You could escort them, perhaps, and see that none goes round to the south door. And then it would be better if the older boys and girls tried to settle down to sleep. They're getting out of hand."

"What do you expect with that wretched little Peter shouting 'Murder!' all over the place?" Emily asked bitterly. "Oh, Richard, I can't believe it's really happening. And that pencil! I saw Caroline High in Church Lane some time before half-past six, when I was standing on the landing looking for you. She looked so queer that I nearly went out to her to ask if I could do anything. She was coming down from the churchyard."

Richard Varney looked very grave.

"There must be some explanation. She *can't* have killed him! But I'm afraid that must wait. Good heavens! Here comes a fresh party. Thank God, at least, that people are getting up here."

He went off to deal with the newcomers, who were

almost at once pounced on by the earlier arrivals and told the story of the body by the south porch. Meanwhile, Emily gradually marshalled her flock ready for the wild, dark walk to the Vicarage.

It was very difficult to gather them all together and, on an impulse, she went down to where Caroline was sitting in silent misery and defiance, with Stephan perched on the end of a pew near by.

"Caroline! Stephan, too! Do come and help me. I'm desperate. The little ones are like eels and they don't want to go to the Vicarage. Neither do their mothers, because they feel that this is the place to hear the news. Half of them are frantic with worry about their husbands and homes, and a few are eaten up with curiosity about the murder."

Caroline looked at her with green eyes that were dull in the soft lamplight.

"Yes, come on!" said Stephan, in a thankful voice. "It's an excellent idea."

"I—I can't," said Caroline.

"Of course you can," said Emily. "You'll feel better if you've something to do and the children know you well, even those who don't go to school."

"But people think I've *murdered* him! I don't know how they could. I hate them all!"

Emily knew that she was perilously near breaking point and merely said briskly:

"Rubbish! They don't really think it, and I don't believe you hate them. They're your own people; you grew up amongst them. Do come, because I've got a splitting head ache and I shall burst into tears in a moment."

Caroline gave her a startled, suddenly not unfriendly look and then, with unexpected energy, sprang up and began to help to gather together the writhing, over-excited children. Stephan also helped, looking, so Emily thought as she tackled the mothers, rather like a queer, untrained sheep-dog. At last they were ready and the whole party marched out of the west door, with Stephan at the head of the procession and Emily and Caroline bringing up the rear. Some of the women shuddered and glanced fearfully over their shoulders as they crossed the churchyard, but the wind was too violent and too bitterly cold for them to linger, and most of them had babies in their arms.

At the Vicarage all was noise and bustle. People were still struggling up the lane after being rescued from their flooded houses and there was an alarming shortage of dry clothes. Emily's first task, when she had more or less disposed of the mothers and children, was to try and find some more, but when she had raked through every cupboard and drawer in the house the supply was hardly adequate.

The dining-room, sitting-room and even Mrs. Sainty's usually carefully guarded and almost impregnable kitchen were crowded with people, all talking and most of them drinking tea. Babies were crying and slightly older children were playing in the hall. Upstairs some attempt was being made to arrange beds for everyone, though it was an almost impossible task and the house was going to be full to over-flowing. Old Mrs. Grief was still wailing about the lost "takings", and Minnie, looking sour and making no attempt to help, was one of the few silent people, with her head bent over a hideous piece of knitting that she had apparently had in her capacious handbag.

The news about the murder had soon spread from the "church people" to the Vicarage ones, and of course the information added to the general upset and unrest. Caroline's face grew more and more white and tense, with a decided look of defiance that was not likely to endear her to people, but, to Emily's unspoken admiration, she worked hard and well, undressing the small children and helping to see them into bed. Many covert glances followed her, for the finding of the silver pencil had been imparted as well, of course. Emily did her best to stem gossip, but it was not easy.

She overheard snatches of disturbing conversation.

"She was nice enough when she was young, but what I say is she's never been the same since she had that posh teaching job in London. Stuck up, and more than that."

"Oh, yes, more than that." And knowing nods. "She's got something in her past, that girl, and it's my belief that Thomas Long knew what it was. My old man heard him in the pub only a day or two ago. Said there were things he could tell and might yet."

"Blackmail. That's what it was, like as not. It's my opinion that blackmailers get what they deserve, but that a girl like that could pick up a great stone and knock his brains out—"

"I should be very careful what you say," said Emily. "Miss High is probably as innocent as the rest of us. The fact that her pencil was found near the body doesn't prove that she murdered him."

She moved away, vaguely disquieted by the look that the two women gave her.

"Oh, Mrs. Varney!" That was Mrs. Sainty, wanting permission to use the best cups, since all the others were in use. Emily gave up trying to preserve Caroline's good name. In any case, her own mind was a turmoil of conflicting thoughts and mounting fear.

"Vicar was in the church. Funny 'e didn't 'ear nothin'."

"Oh, God!" thought Emily. "I hate all this!" And her fear increased.

When she, Stephan and Caroline went back to the church through the roaring darkness Dr. Love had arrived and had examined the body. They met him, Mr. Pike and Colonel Pashley carrying it round to the vestry door on an improvised stretcher.

Caroline slipped away silently, Emily hoped into the warmth and light of the church, but Stephan and Emily herself followed the men.

"*Was* it murder?" Stephan asked briskly, as one who expects the worst and doesn't mind very much.

"Oh, certainly," said Dr. Love, as they entered the small musty little room and the shrouded body was put down carefully in a corner. "At a rough guess I should say that he was very drunk—probably more than he's ever been—and someone saw him hovering there near the south porch and biffed him one. We've got the stone safely, but it won't show finger-prints. Much too rough a surface. Anyhow, it was a bitter evening and whoever touched it was almost certainly wearing gloves."

"But," Emily looked at him with shadowed dark eyes, "if

that was so wouldn't there have been blood on—on someone? Quite a lot of blood?"

"Well, actually there wasn't so much. But I think the stone was thrown from quite a distance. Someone had a good aim. So there was no danger of it getting on their clothes. I'll have to make a more careful examination, of course. In fact, I'd better get down to it now. Your husband says he found the body at twenty to seven and he didn't think that death had occurred very long before. I'd certainly put the time at between six and six-thirty. Can't get much nearer than that, because of the intense cold tonight. But it can't have been much earlier than six, as he was in the Roaring Bull till twenty to, I'm told."

"I'd better get through to the police at once, don't you think so, Doctor?" That was Mr. Valentine Pike, reluctant, but determined to do his duty, and also determined to see that no one else took charge of the fascinating affair until the moment when the police regrettably walked in.

"Well, yes," agreed Dr. Love. "You'd better tell them all about it, but it doesn't look as though they'll be able to get here for a day or two. The water seems to have gone some distance inland and I think we're pretty well surrounded."

Mr. Pike brightened visibly.

"I thought that myself. And I'm perfectly willing to do what I can until the police manage to get here."

Dr. Love said "Hum!" rather unenthusiastically, and Mr. Pike, accompanied by Colonel Pashley, went off to the Vicarage, while Emily and Stephan entered the church. A little order had now been made out of the original chaos and a good many of the young people were settling down for the night on the hard pews, after a meal of bread and cheese, chocolate and apples. Quite a number of people had had the forethought to snatch up a loaf or some fruit as the flood waters rose, so no one was actually hungry, though food was going to be a problem very shortly. A few, who had taken the flood warning seriously, had even had small bags ready packed.

Emily glanced round quickly and saw her husband talking to old Mrs. Gotts, whose bright eyes and beaky little nose were sticking up out of a cocoon of blankets. Caroline, she saw with relief, was there, standing alone near one of the stoves.

The talk was still of murder, mixed with anxious speculations about the fate of many different homes. But the murder seemed to take first place, Emily realized with some surprise and a great deal of disquiet. She did not like the general air of avid curiosity and uneasiness.

She went about quietly, doing what she could to make people comfortable, and was near the back of the church when the west door opened and Mr. Pike and Colonel Pashley came back.

"They bin to phone the p'lice!" a village woman said shrilly, and again Emily felt a stab at her heart. How had the woman realized that?

"An' they bin movin' the body, too!" said another voice.

"Do the p'lice come they'll soon get the murderer!" said the first woman. "Not nice nor pleasant it isn't, feeling there's a murderer among us. They'll get a boat, like as not, an' —"

"Are the police coming when the water goes down a

little?" Emily asked clearly. There seemed no point in trying to hush matters up; worse rumours would only grow out of the uncertainty.

Mr. Pike looked round him.

"I'm afraid not. Not for some time, anyhow. The telephone lines are dead and we're quite cut off here in the church and Vicarage."

There was a startled silence and then someone cried shrilly:

"But there's bin a murder! Do there be a murder there must be p'lice!"

"Well, the Colonel and I thought . . ." Mr. Pike looked round again. "The Colonel and I thought that we'd better investigate the matter to the best of our ability." He had been forced to include the Colonel, who was a man of considerable personality. It went against the grain, but he was quite sure that he, with a brain that was well trained in detective matters, would hit on the solution to the problem. "After all, a murder isn't the sort of thing that can be allowed to remain unsolved, and by the time the police get here . . . Well, we thought—"

"A very good idea, that's what I say!" cried Mrs. Gotts, with tremendous enthusiasm. "Someone's got to, 'aven't they now?"

"Here, I say!" said Stephan. "It's true, of course. But still I don't see why . . ." He liked the Colonel well enough, but thought Mr. Pike a bore and rather a fool, with his passion for detective stories. The fellow needn't think he was going to act as a sort of Assistant Commissioner.

There was a murmur of disagreement. Everyone was

listening intently and it was evident that most people would welcome an investigation of some kind. On the whole Mr. Pike and the Colonel were well respected.

"Us doesn't want to be murdered in our beds!" said old Mrs. Gotts, banging the back of the pew suddenly with a hymn-book. No one had thought her capable of getting her hands out of the blankets. "Let the gen'lemen find out 'oo done it!"

"Well, first of all," said Dr. Love, who had emerged from the vestry, "let's find out if *they've* got alibis."

"My dear sir!" Mr. Pike flushed indignantly.

"Merely a matter of form," said the doctor genially. "Where were you between six and a quarter to seven this evening?"

"I was at home with my wife until about five past six," said Mr. Pike, looking round for confirmation and finding it in his dull, plain spouse's eager nod. "And furthermore there's Barbara Woodrow to back me up. Fetched my overcoat and hat for me, didn't you, Barbara? And I remarked on the time and said I'd be back long before dinner."

"Oh, yes, sir!" Barbara, a young village girl employed by the Pikes, spoke eagerly from her seat on an upturned box. "I remember it was five past six on the hall clock, and the news was on, too."

Mr. Pike looked round triumphantly.

"Well, I got to the pub at just on ten past, as half a dozen people can testify, I expect. No time for murder, eh?"

"And the Colonel?" asked Dr. Love cheerfully. Colonel Pashley said amiably:

"I was with my wife and Mrs. Abel-Otty till six-fifteen or

thereabouts, then I walked straight to the Roaring Bull for a quick one. After that I was walking back with Rust's young son, who was wanting advice about a gun. Always out on the marshes, as you know. You can ask him. We heard the flood coming—saw it, too, by Jove!—and he grabbed one boat and I grabbed another."

"So that's clear enough," said Mr. Pike. "But I suppose we can hardly start tonight. Time we were off and had another try at getting to the further houses, though the wind's so bad it's almost impossible. Coming, Pashley?"

The Colonel nodded and they went off again.

"One can't help admiring them," Emily thought grudgingly, as she leaned tiredly against a pillar. Then she was suddenly galvanized into violent awareness, for Caroline High had darted out into the clear space near the west door. Her face was distorted by fear and rage and her voice took on a ghastly, hysterical note.

"I didn't do it, I tell you! I know you all think I did! He was lying there—I saw him, that was all, when I was going into the church. I hated him, but I wouldn't have murdered him. I didn't! I didn't! And I wish *I* was dead!"

Then she crumpled up into a heap, her hair very bright against the tiles, and there was a long silence in which Emily felt the worst fear of her life creeping up her spine.

" 'Course she murdered 'im! She's got spirit, that girl! An' 'e well deserved it!" said old Mrs. Gotts, thumping so violently with the aged hymn-book that pages flew out in all directions.

Chapter 4
MR. PIKE STARTS INVESTIGATING

IT WAS eleven o'clock before all was more or less quiet in the church. Emily had given Caroline High a mild sedative and had tucked her up on a small mattress in a corner. Mrs. Gotts had gone to sleep at last, worn out after all the excitement, and most people were disposed of in some measure, though comfort was by no means to be the keynote of that strange night in the church.

Emily and Richard came together at last, both nearly dropping with strain and weariness. Emily, usually so careful of her appearance, knew that her hair was in a hopeless tangle and her face totally devoid of make-up. Her stockings were laddered and her clothes and hands dirty. Richard was in little better shape, though his cold seemed astonishingly better.

"Had no time to think about it," he assured her. They leaned against a pillar in a shadowy corner and Emily thrust a cold, roughened hand into his.

"Let's go back to the Vicarage, Richard. We can't do anything here and we must have some strength for tomorrow. I feel"—and she shivered—"it's going to be much worse than today!"

"You're probably right," her husband agreed. "Well, let's go and find some corner. There's really nothing more we can do until morning, though I feel that I ought to be out in one of the boats."

"They've given up till daylight. All of them," said Emily,

who had had the news from Dr. Love. "The wind's too bad and the water's too deep. Oh, Richard! It's like some awful nightmare! I keep on thinking of how the village looked before dark; all the little roofs, the curving flint walls and the marsh so vast and colourless. And now—out there in the blackness—"

"It's no good. Stop thinking about it. A really surprising number of people are safe already."

With a few last words to Dr. Love and Mr. and Mrs. Abel-Otty, who had made a sort of bivouac in a corner with hassocks and rugs, they went out for the last time into the night. The wind still screamed about the church, but the sky was now bright with stars and scattered with flying banks of cloud. There was even a trace of a moon.

Quietness reigned at the Vicarage, too, as they crept along the hall, though people stirred and muttered in their uncomfortable sleep. Mrs. Sainty met them in the kitchen doorway, looking neater and more composed than almost anyone on that night of trouble and horror. She seemed quite to have recovered from her original shock.

Finger on lips, she greeted them with relief.

"I'm glad you've come back—right glad! There was no call to sleep in that damp church and your reverence with a cold. I've kept you a mattress in the little spare room. It was the best I could do with them coming in in dozens, so wet and upset. But there're blankets, and I've put you some tea in a flask and left sandwiches."

Emily found herself shamefully near to tears. She had certainly never expected such luxury that night.

"Oh, Mrs. Sainty, how wonderful of you! But we

shouldn't be any better off than anyone else. Don't you think—"

"Oh, it's not all that grand. It's a hard mattress, I'm afraid, and the room's as cold as a tomb, having no electric fire."

"Where are you sleeping?"

"Oh, I've my bed by the kitchen fire. I've got several others in there, but they'll not disturb me. Get upstairs, the pair of you. You look ready to collapse!"

"We're going now. But we must be up as soon as it's light. Before, perhaps. There'll be so much to do if the water goes down."

"It won't. Not tomorrow. There'll be another high tide and the wind's still coming from the north like a demon. It's my belief that we'll get no outside help before it drops, though there's some who expect help any minute. And there's that nasty murder to deal with."

"Yes." Before Emily's tired eyes rose a vision of Caroline High's distorted face. "Yes, there's going to be dreadful trouble."

"Well, don't you be worrying now. Get upstairs and have your hot drink. Good night, Mrs. Varney. Good night, sir."

The little spare room was indeed small—little more than a slip of a boxroom and never dignified by the presence of a bed. It was, as Mrs. Sainty had said, bitterly cold, but it was quiet and empty. They ate and drank in silence, and then partially undressed and lay down on the hard mattress.

In the darkness, relaxing gradually in the warmth, Emily thought gratefully:

"At least we're together, and I won't worry. There must be some explanation and perhaps that inquisitive Mr. Pike will find it out. Perhaps it somehow wasn't murder, after all, but an accident." Her husband's arm encircled her warmly and she moved nearer to him, some of her fear evaporating.

The wind still blew, but she no longer heard it.

She awoke during the night, momentarily glad to shake off a nightmare in which she herself was accused of murder. But reality, she discovered, as she lay listening once more to the unceasing wind, was not so very much better than the dream. She had *not* been accused yet, but, remembering the covert looks of the two gossiping women, she thought uneasily that it was not beyond the bounds of possibility that such a thing might happen. It might easily, in fact, if Thomas Long, his unpleasant tongue loosened by increasing amounts of drink, had hinted that he knew something about her that she wished to keep a secret.

"But he can't have done," Emily said to herself in the darkness, and she moved nearer to her husband's warm, sleeping body. "The whole thing would be absurd. No one would commit murder to keep a silly secret like mine. People will have *some* sense."

But she lay there remembering how she had wandered about the lonely house at the fatal time. No alibi whatever. Undoubtedly Mr. Pike would try to investigate every channel and the result might be humiliating to say the least.

Once her mind had begun to get hold of the problem she felt that she would never sleep again. It must have been about twenty-five to seven when Betony had come . . .

Betony! She remembered with sudden, heart-stopping vividness the child's haunted air, her coldness and her shaken voice. She had not thought much about it at the time, being so wholly occupied with worrying about Richard. But was it possible that the child had seen something in the churchyard? Or perhaps she had only sensed something. Betony was sensitive and aware. Could she possibly . . . Could that have been why . . . ?

"We'll have to ask her, I suppose," she thought with distaste, remembering her last sight of Betony. She had been sitting in one of the pews beside her mother, looking more than usually fine-drawn, but apparently blessedly absorbed in the poems of W. B. Yeats. Emily had said good night to her, and Betony had looked up with a dazed but by no means unhappy air. She was reading *The Hosting of the Sidhe.*

> *"The host is riding from Knocknarea*
> *And over the grave of Clooth-na-Bare;*
> *Caoilte tossing his burning hair,*
> *And Niamh calling, 'Away, come away;*
> *Empty your heart of its mortal dream,*
> *The winds awaken . . .'."*

Oh, yes, Betony had been far, far removed from a flood-surrounded church on a low Norfolk hill; far from murder and pain and fear. She could not, surely, understand the poem, but it obviously delighted her. She had scarcely seen Emily, though she had said good night.

The child had been touched enough; it was her father

who lay in the vestry. Was there the faintest hope that she need not be questioned and upset?

Emily's common sense came to her aid.

"She'll have to say what she knows; if she knows anything."

But the thought of the dreamy, poetry-loving child being torn back to a decidedly cruel world made her move violently on the narrow mattress and Richard awoke and murmured in her ear:

"Don't think about it now. Get some sleep. You'll need it."

And somehow, miraculously, Emily drifted off again and did not dream at all.

She awoke to find Mrs. Sainty, fully dressed and almost as neat as usual, standing above her with a small tray.

"Oh, we oughtn't to have tea!" she said sleepily, and Mrs. Sainty retorted:

"I see no reason why not. There's not a soul going to do without it. We're making gallons of it."

It was a dim, grey morning; the north wind still blew and the air was icy.

"What's happening?" Emily asked as she took the tray, sitting up uncomfortably on the hard mattress.

"Not much yet. There've been a couple of planes over, but I shouldn't think they could see much, it's that gloomy. Breakfast will be the first real problem. We've got to get some food from somewhere before the day's over. Some of the men are on the move already; I saw them going past the gate."

"We ought to be up, too," said Emily, handing one of the

old flowered cups to her husband, who was still blinking sleepily.

"The water's still as high as ever and some of those poor souls still trapped in their homes. But there doesn't seem much anyone can do while the wind's as bad as this." Mrs. Sainty shuddered and departed quickly.

From the spare-room window as she dressed hurriedly Emily looked out over the flood waters. The red-roofed houses looked more than ever like arks; she could just see in the gloom a boat moving slowly along where the marsh road should have been, and here and there the higher brick and flint walls stood up out of the water. But it was only here and there. As far as she could judge by the height of the water against the houses the flood was in places all of fifteen feet deep.

The Vicarage was filled with noise; children were shouting and crying, doors banged, footsteps came and went unceasingly.

Richard Varney dressed and went off to see how affairs were in the church, and Emily, feeling more tired, grubby and dispirited than ever before in her life, set to work to help with the breakfast. It had been impossible to wash, for several people had been sleeping in the bathroom and some were still there.

The Vicarage's well-stocked storeroom had been ransacked by Mrs. Sainty and people were making do with whatever cold food there was, some of it unpalatable on such a bitter morning. There was no gas or electricity for cooking, but there were kettles on all the fires so that there would be a constant supply of boiling water.

The scene was indescribably sordid; the house was littered with bedding and possessions, a child had been sick in the hall and another had had an "accident" on the stairs. But on the whole people were good-tempered and patient, though it was clear to Emily that Mrs. Grief was going to cause trouble. She was in a bad mood and was determined to do her best to stir those around her into the same state. Minnie was little better, for her grumbling never ceased and she always seemed to be under Emily's feet as she hurried about trying to see that the younger children got something suitable to eat. Fortunately some of the cows from the marsh had found their way to safety on the hill and they had already been milked, so there was fresh milk for all the children, including the older ones in the church, which was a big help.

The main topics of conversation were the state of the houses below, the possible fate of relations and friends not yet accounted for, and the murder. Emily felt uneasily that tension was growing over the murder and she blamed it largely on Mrs. Grief and some of the other elderly women, for they were talking a great deal too much, in rather uncontrolled voices, about the danger of being murdered themselves. Unless something intervened things were going to be very unpleasant on Church Hill while the body lay in the vestry and the murderer was at large.

As for the missing people, Richard's first task that morning was to try and make a complete list of those saved, and then, by a process of elimination, it would be possible to know what still had to be done in the way of rescue. Some, undoubtedly, were dead. Four bodies had been taken out of the water already and these lay in one of the Vicarage outbuildings behind a locked door.

When Emily went up to the church—glad of the walk through the bitter, uninviting air—the roll call was taking place. The names so typical of Norfolk echoed through the crowded and littered building.

Emily found Caroline at her side as she stood near the west door. The girl looked ghastly, but was apparently in control of herself.

The short, staccato names followed one after another: Rust, Gotts, Musk, Joy, Cod, Lines . . .

"Oh, God! Listen to them!" said Caroline High. "Cod, Herring, Mackerel, Gotts! How I loathe and detest Norfolk!" The break in her voice showed that she was not so calm as she looked.

"I can't say that I like the names," Emily said quietly. "But I certainly like Norfolk, though it is in some ways so slow and harsh."

"Except for your name," said Caroline. "Varney! I like that. And it is Norfolk, isn't it?"

"How are things going, do you think?" Emily asked, thinking it best for her to talk.

Caroline looked at her.

"Do *you* think I murdered that abominable man?"

"No. I'm sure you've got too much control and common sense. Besides, it could never have been worth it."

"You don't know. Everyone's saying . . . They're saying he had something on me. He was hinting it. They all know. He couldn't hold his tongue just lately."

"And had he?"

Caroline's white face flamed into sudden colour, so that she looked beautiful as well as desperate.

"I hated him!" she said and, turning on her heel, walked away towards a group of the younger children.

Stephan came up laconically. He, in company with everyone else, looked dirty and weary. There was a hint of dark stubble on his chin.

"Have a nice night, Aunt Emily?"

"Better than might have been expected," said Emily. "I feel guilty. How did you fare?"

"Oh, so-so. Might have been worse. Look here! It's beginning to go round that Mr. Abel-Otty committed the murder. That's the latest, but the place is seething with rumours and there's a trace of panic that I don't like."

"I don't like it, either," agreed Emily, remembering the atmosphere at the Vicarage. "But why on earth Mr. Abel-Otty?"

"Oh, someone went down to the Vicarage just now and came back with the tale that Mrs. Grief is putting it about that he came up to the churchyard last night about the time of the murder."

"But that's nonsense. He came to see Richard. I suppose she saw him coming up the lane?"

"Yes, she did. I said that, of course. But they'll believe anything at the moment. Anyhow, there are two people who are going to enjoy themselves; old Pike and the Colonel, though the Colonel's a bit of an also ran, seems to me. They're down there in the chancel, drawing up tables of people's movements or something and making lists. Hell! I wish this bloody water would go down!"

Emily wished it, too, as she walked round the church, speaking to people and trying to be reassuring. But Dr. Love and some of the other men had been up on the church tower and had reported that the flood waters seemed to stretch for miles behind Marshton. No doubt the Army, or other rescuers, would get through presently, but meanwhile they were marooned on the hill containing church and Vicarage and a few fields.

"Might as well be on a desert island," thought Emily, wondering anxiously how the rest of the coast had fared.

Betony was sitting curled up in the corner of a pew, her uncombed fair hair hanging forward over the pages of a small book. She was writing busily.

"Good morning, Betony," said Emily, and the child looked up, startled.

"Good morning, Mrs. Varney."

"You look very busy."

Betony shut the little book and put it carefully in her pocket.

"I was writing my diary, Mrs. Varney. I always keep it up to date and it's something to do."

"Yes, it must be very boring sitting about here. Why don't you take some of the children outside and play some games? It's very cold and windy, but it would be better to run about for a few minutes."

Betony went off rather reluctantly, but was soon to be seen departing in the company of several seven- and eight-year-olds. Emily envied her. The atmosphere in the church, while still chilly, was anything but pleasant.

Suddenly she found Mr. Pike at her elbow.

"Mrs. Varney, I wonder if you can help me? There are rumours flying round that Mr. Abel-Otty was in the churchyard some time after six o'clock. He denies it strenuously and says he came up Church Lane only as far as the Vicarage, because he wanted to see your husband. When he found that he was out he says he waited for a while and was with you when the flood came."

"Yes, that's perfectly correct." Emily looked at him with some distaste. "He arrived just as Betony was leaving. She came up to borrow a book. It was just on twenty to seven. I remember looking at my watch."

"Twenty to seven?" Mr. Pike's tone was so portentous that Emily jumped.

"Yes. It can't have been a minute before. My watch is always right. Betony had been with me for about five minutes and—"

"But I've just slipped down to see Mrs. Grief, and the old girl insists that she and her daughter saw him pass their side windows at the foot of the lane at six-fifteen precisely. They were listening to the wireless and the news was just over."

"But—" Emily's brain felt as though it would never work clearly again.

"Mrs. Grief swears it, and, though she's inclined to be a mischief-maker, I shouldn't think she'd invent that. Mr. Abel-Otty himself says he didn't take note of the time. He had been writing and just put aside his work and went up to try and see your husband about some maps."

"Well, if the Griefs are correct he must have been doing *something*, but he'd hardly have wanted to linger in that awful wind." Emily pushed her untidy dark hair back from her forehead. "Good gracious! It's nonsense! Why should he murder Thomas Long?"

"The rumour is that Mr. Long was trying to blackmail him. Was threatening to tell his wife that he was carrying on with the village lovelies."

"But . . ." Emily paused, her distaste mounting, though she knew it was unreasonable. "Everyone knew that he liked to notice pretty girls. Even I knew, though I do my best to hear as little gossip as possible. Sorry to sound smug, but I loathed some of the talk that went on."

"Everyone knew but his wife, it seems. And though they may gossip the village folk aren't bad really and wouldn't have gone to her with a tale. God knows," said Mr. Pike fervently, "one couldn't blame him, married to that stony, houseproud woman, but murder is murder and—"

"So it is," Emily agreed, rather tartly. "And I can't feel he'd murder anyone to keep the news from his wife."

"Don't forget she's got money, though she doesn't spend much of it. He doesn't make much with those books of his and maybe he's counting—well, he wouldn't want her to leave him if she felt she had cause. She looks a hard woman, and—"

"An unpleasant business—murder!" said Colonel Pashley quietly, appearing beside them. "I think we'll have to start at the beginning and question everyone possible and then try and put it all together."

"Yes," agreed Mr. Pike, with some relish. "We must start with all the people who were anywhere near the churchyard between six and a quarter to seven, or who could have been. With all due respect, Mrs. Varney, where were you at that time?"

Emily flushed, but it was no use trying to snub him.

"I was alone in the Vicarage for two-thirds of the time as you probably know, Mr. Pike. As the whole village probably knows."

"And you saw no one at all until Betony Long arrived?"

"Well!" Emily hesitated. "I was standing at an upper window watching for my husband when I saw Miss High coming down the Lane. That must have been at about twenty-five past or half-past six. I can't say exactly. There can be no harm in telling you that, as she says she saw the body. In fact it's a wonder that Mrs. Grief hasn't reported seeing her passing their windows."

"It seems that both Mrs. Grief and her daughter went back into the shop and were absorbed in arranging some new stock that arrived during the afternoon. The High girl says she was going into the church, but there seems no sense in that. She hardly ever goes to church on Sundays, let alone on such a bad week-day evening. And after you saw Miss High?"

"Well, as I told you, Betony called at about twenty-five to seven and just as she was going Mr. Abel-Otty came." On an impulse Emily added earnestly, speaking more to the Colonel than to Mr. Pike: "The child came through the churchyard and did seem very distressed and upset, but I put it down to the fact that she was cold and her father had apparently been bullying her the previous night. She must have passed to the north on the footpath, but I do think it possible that she saw something. I hate to think of her being questioned and upset again, but still it seems necessary—"

"Yes." The Colonel looked grave. "It was getting dark, of course, but she might have seen something, though by the time she must have been about the murder must have been over and the murderer had probably gone. According to Miss High, it was between twenty past and twenty-five past six that she saw the body. But—there's something else worrying you?"

"Well, if the child *did* see anything she might be in danger from the murderer," said Emily. "Still, if she came through the churchyard it would almost certainly have been too late to see anything—unless perhaps the body."

Dr. Love suddenly loomed up beside them.

"My God! These rumours! They can't all have done it, and, by the way, while we're on the subject, I've got a foolproof alibi. I was out at Dyke Farm until nearly six and then I drove back like a fiend and rushed into my surgery. Stayed there signing forms and suchlike for a constant stream of people until the flood came and caught us all napping. Mrs. Varney, the latest is that your nephew had a hand in it."

Emily jumped and her heart seemed to turn over. "Stephan! How absurd! Why on earth should *he* murder Thomas Long?"

"Goodness knows, except that they apparently had a quarrel and he was heard by two men from the village to say that he'd kill him if he said something or other again."

"Oh, but—people say that sort of thing."

"Of course they do. But it goes hard when a murder

follows. Did you know that they quarrelled?"

"I had heard about it, but Stephan never mentioned it. He's touchy just now and I didn't think it necessary or wise to question him."

"Well, I'll have to see him, of course. Probably he wasn't near the churchyard," said Mr. Pike.

"He was at the pub when I got there just after six-twenty," remarked the Colonel.

"Just come," said Mr. Pike. "Said he'd been for one of those long walks of his. Oh, well, no doubt it's nonsense, but we can't leave any stone unturned. Mrs. Varney, is there any small room at the Vicarage where we can conduct our investigations?"

"I'll try and clear the little study," said Emily. "People slept there, but they don't need it in the daytime."

The Colonel coughed.

"Er—Mrs. Varney, we were wondering—very unpleasant business this, but still—we were wondering—"

"Yes?" Emily bristled less when talking to the Colonel.

"You write shorthand, don't you? My wife says you used to take notes when you were Secretary of the Women's Institute. We ought to have a full record to hand to the police, and it would be fairer to take down exactly what is said. People *may* object, but in view of the general strong feeling they may realize that it would be wiser to help all they can. I don't like—"

"None of us likes it," said Emily. "But you can't force people to allow their statements to be recorded."

"No, but it *would* be best, don't you think? Even if the rescue parties get through there's another high tide expected, and by the time we get in touch with the police—"

"Oh, well, I'll help you all I can," Emily agreed. "I'll go straight down now and see about the study, and then you can start."

She made her way slowly and rather draggingly up the south aisle and came suddenly face to face with her husband. He looked so concerned that she stopped abruptly.

"Richard! Has something else happened? Why are you looking like that?"

"Oh, there's nothing really," said the Vicar. "I've just heard that they've got the party from Marsh Farm and are bringing them up. Half dead with cold, poor things. And—Emily, you haven't found a letter?"

"A *letter?* What letter?"

"A letter I had in my jacket pocket. I must have shot it out without noticing it. I can't find it anywhere."

Chapter 5
WHO WAS IN THE CHURCHYARD?

FOR a moment Emily stared at him, while her whole body seemed to go cold.

"I haven't seen a letter, Richard. I don't think you dropped it in the spare room. Was it very important?"

"Oh, well, not so very," said her husband, but his troubled face belied his words. "It'll turn up, I suppose," and then, with a brief, rather unseeing smile, he passed on.

As Emily went out through the west door and along the narrow path that joined the through track from the main road to Church Lane her mind shrank from the implications of the few words. A letter! Richard had had a letter that he hated on the previous morning. He had crumpled it up and thrust it into his pocket and later she had half-suspected that it might have been from Thomas Long. And yet that had been pure speculation—instinct. Probably she was quite wrong and the missing letter had nothing whatever to do with the murdered man. All the same her deep sense of uneasiness increased.

To make matters worse the wind was blowing more violently than ever and cold rain was beginning to fall. She had tied a scarf over her hair and she wore a warm coat, but the wind seemed to go through her bones. By the time she reached the Vicarage gate there was hail mingled with the rain. It bounced on the top of the brick and flint wall and lay in white beads on the lawn.

"Oh, God!" she thought, remembering the people still

trapped in the isolated houses and farms. "Let the weather improve!"

As she hesitated at the gate she could see a little party coming slowly up the lane. There would be an immediate need for hot water and hot drinks . . . brandy . . . food.

She flew into the house, picking her way through children and dogs to find Mrs. Sainty in the kitchen.

When she had done all she could she made her way to the little study. A fire burned there and bedding and other possessions were littered about, but the room was empty. It was too small to have much attraction; most people seemed to prefer to huddle in groups in the larger rooms. Murder still seemed to be the main topic of conversation.

"There'll be someone else for it . . ." she had caught. "There always is. Never content with one, a murderer isn't. After all, what I says is you can only hang once."

The hail was banging against the window and from it she could just see the wind-whipped flood water. No boat would be able to make its way into that northerly gale from the slight uplands further inland.

Quickly she opened the desk and arranged chairs, and before she had finished Mr. Pike and the Colonel were there, the former still looking rather self-important, the latter much troubled.

"Rather hate this, you know," mumbled the Colonel. "But the people do seem to want it. They'll feel better when they know that something is being done. Miss High is coming up now. She's got guts, that girl. Always liked her, in spite of that grim, tragic air. Used to know her when she was a little thing. Used to see her bird-watching out on the marshes. Pretty kid, and could be a beautiful woman now, if—"

"I can't stand that cold type," said Mr. Pike briskly.

"Oh, but she isn't really!" Emily said involuntarily.

The Colonel nodded.

"Agree with you, Mrs. Varney. Something happened to her while she was away in London. It stuck out a mile when she came back. 'Tisn't natural for a young woman to look like an iceberg. Sorry she's in trouble now. She's had to put up with enough."

"She'll have to put up with more if she did murder that chap," said Mr. Pike. "And so far she's the most suspect."

They settled themselves with pens and paper and almost at once there was a knock at the door. When it opened Caroline High came slowly and with some dignity into the room. She still wore the unbecoming borrowed clothes and her face was white and tense, but she had an air of cold, still dignity and control.

"Sit by the fire, Caroline," said Emily, pitying her deeply. "This is a horrible affair, but—"

"I'd sooner stand, thank you," said Caroline, unmoved. "What did you want to ask me? I've told you all I know already."

Mr. Pike promptly took charge.

"It will be best if you make a clear statement, Miss High, and Mrs. Varney here will take it down in shorthand. Once we have everything clear we shall be well on the way to solving this most distressing business."

Caroline stood with one hand on the back of a chair and her knuckles were white.

"I can't tell you much. I didn't murder Thomas Long. It was a horrible evening and I was tired of being in the house alone. I thought I'd just go up to the church, so I walked up Church Lane and across the churchyard towards the south porch. I knew that that was the door that is always open in winter. I saw the body as I approached and went and bent over it. That must have been when I dropped my pencil. It was in my top pocket. I—I saw at once that he was dead, and I—I felt so sick and queer I turned round and went straight back. I kept on thinking I was going to faint, but I got home all right. I knew I ought to tell someone, but somehow I couldn't. I had a drop of brandy in the house and I drank it and sat by the fire. Then the flood came and I dashed upstairs, and I was lucky enough to be rescued before very long."

"What time did you go up to the churchyard?"

"I—I haven't really the least idea. But it was well after six. About a quarter past, I should think, or twenty past. I walked very fast and it wouldn't take more than five minutes to get up there. I came back straight away."

"Mrs. Varney says she was at an upper window of the Vicarage and saw you returning some time between twenty-five past and half-past six."

Caroline flashed Emily a quick look.

"That would be about the time. I did notice that it was twenty-five to seven when I got back into my sitting-room. I—I walked very slowly on the way back."

"But what we want to establish, my dear young lady," said the Colonel gently, "is what time you left home. Did you meet anyone?"

73

Caroline suddenly flushed deeply.

"Yes, I did. I didn't remember till the middle of the night. That is, I saw him, but—but I'm not sure if he saw me."

"Oh! Was it Mr. Abel-Otty? He is said to have left home and gone up Church Lane just at six-fifteen."

"No, it wasn't Mr. Abel-Otty." Caroline spoke with evident reluctance. "I didn't see him at all."

"Who, then?"

"I saw Mr. Stephan Varney. He—as I left the house I saw him turn out of Church Lane and go striding away along the marsh road towards the junction of the main road. You know how fast he walks? I was still at the gate, but he had his head slightly bent against the wind and his coat collar up. He might not have seen me."

Emily had stifled a cry, and Mr. Pike said swiftly and with satisfaction:

"You saw Mr. Stephan Varney coming out of Church Lane?"

Caroline nodded.

"Yes. Why, is it so very surprising? After all, he lives there. He had probably just come down from the Vicarage—"

Mr. Pike looked across at Emily.

"Did he call in after his walk?"

"No," said Emily slowly, her heart very heavy. "No, I didn't see him until he came home just before my husband, when he said he'd ended his walk at the Roaring Bull."

"Well, we'll have to wait till later for his account of the matter," said Mr. Pike, lighting his pipe and puffing furiously. He turned back to Caroline. "And you didn't see

Mr. Abel-Otty in front of you?"

Caroline frowned.

"I didn't see anyone else. Should he have been?"

"Well, Mrs. Grief and her daughter swear that they saw him starting up Church Lane just at six-fifteen. You can't have been more than a minute or two behind him."

"I didn't see him," Caroline repeated with certainty.

"Well, now, Miss High, there's one other thing. Why were you thinking of going into the church?"

Caroline flushed again and her voice took on a new stiffness and defiance.

"Can't I go into the church if I want to?"

"Well, of course. But doesn't it strike you as strange that you should say you were intending to go into the church on such a bad, darkening evening, when you rarely even attend the services?"

"You can think what you like about that," said Caroline coldly. "I was *going into the church*. And if I can't help you any more I think I'd better go and help with the children, if their mothers will let me near them. Probably I'm regarded as a malevolent influence," and she turned on her heel.

"Well!" Mr. Pike puffed harder than ever when she had gone, and Emily thought that in future she would never be able to bear the smell of a pipe. Mr. Abel-Otty had been smoking furiously on the previous evening and it was rapidly growing to be associated in her mind with uncomfortable and terrifying events. "We'll have to question your nephew, Mrs. Varney. Perhaps, of course, he called in here for something and you never heard him."

Emily shook her head.

"That's not possible. I would have heard him. But there must be some explanation."

Just then there was another knock at the door and it opened a crack. A timid voice said:

"Could I speak to you, Mr. Pike, sir?"

"Why, yes, Mrs. Herring. What is it?" Mr. Pike, not best pleased, looked up from the complicated chart he had made.

"Well, sir, I do be hating all this talk of murder, but it seems it's a question of who went through the churchyard after six o'clock and I *saw* someone."

"You saw someone?"

"Yes. You see, sir, I live next door to the Longs, as you know. Not that I've ever had much to do with them, Mrs. Long being standoffish like, on account of her husband not making it easy to know people, probably, poor woman. I hate to say anything against her, when she's had trouble enough. But I saw her—"

"You saw her? Where?" Mr. Pike looked at the woman with sharp interest. She was middle-aged and very respectable, but just now she looked dishevelled and unhappy.

"I was drawing the curtains in the front bedroom, sir. It was such a dismal evening and I thought the daylight'd be better shut out. It was ten past six; I know that because the chiming clock's ten minutes slow exactly and it struck six at that very moment. Mrs. Long came up from the marsh road, and I thought, 'She's been to the pub looking for that husband of hers; *I* wouldn't worry about him, poisonous as a snake!' But she didn't turn in at her gate. She stopped a moment and then went up the path to the churchyard."

"Can you swear to that? Did you watch her?"

"No. I mean I can swear she went up the path, but I wasn't that interested and I only remembered I'd seen her this morning, with all the worry an' all. I just saw her start up and then I drew the curtains on that horrible windy evening and went downstairs to stoke up the fire. But I had to tell someone. Maybe I should have gone to her, but—"

"That's all right. We'll see Mrs. Long," the Colonel said reassuringly. "Perhaps if you can find her you'll ask her to come along and speak to us?"

"Oh, I can find her. She's down here now getting a hot drink for Betony. Seems the child's got a pain in her stomach, and no wonder."

Mrs. Herring departed, and Mr. Pike made an entry on his chart, remarking:

"Another suspect, you see! This gets interesting."

"Was *everyone* in the churchyard between six and a quarter to seven?" asked Emily. Things seemed to her more nightmarish than ever.

Mrs. Long arrived within a couple of minutes. She looked ghastly, as though she had recently been crying.

"You wanted me, Mr. Pike?" It was noticeable that she did not call him "sir". However bad she looked, Mrs. Long seemed already less spiritless than she had been while her husband was alive.

"Yes, Mrs. Long. We have—er—we have information that leads us to think that you went up to the churchyard last night at ten minutes past six. Did you, in fact, go there?"

Mrs. Long burst into wild sobs, so that her whole body shook.

"No, I didn't! I never went near the horrible place and anyone who says I did is telling a lie. I just felt restless, because Thomas hadn't come in for his tea and Betony should have been home from school by then. I don't know what made me start up the path, but I didn't go far, I swear. It was a horrible evening and bitterly cold and I—I turned round and came back before I'd gone more than fifty yards. I never knew that Thomas was lying there until Peter Love came in with the terrible news, and—and—"

"But you cannot have been fond of your husband?"

Mrs. Long stopped crying.

"Fond of him? No, I was afraid of him, and I hated him, too, for what he was doing to the child. He seemed to get more wicked every day that passed, and all the drink he was taking! Heaven knows where he put it and where he got the money for it. He didn't make much with the garage, especially in the winter. He never used to drink much; just started suddenly and seemed not to be able to stop. But I worried about him; can't you understand that? He wasn't bad when we were married; I didn't always hate him. And as for murdering him—I didn't—"

"She could never have thrown the stone," said the Colonel, in a low voice. "It must have taken a good aim."

"She could, you know," said Mr. Pike, equally low. "She's tough enough and probably has good muscles with doing her own housework and washing. She *could* have done it."

"I don't know *who* did it!" said Mrs. Long, wailing again. "But he was there in front of me. A nice young man, and in trouble himself, apparently, what with his eye and everything. But if it's a question of people who were near the churchyard *he* was there."

"*Who?*"

"Why, Mr. Stephan Varney. Striding along up the hill above me he was. He was nearly at the kissing-gate when I saw him."

"Oh!" Mr. Pike made the exclamation very weighty. He allowed Mrs. Long to depart and then turned to the Colonel.

"He did go through, evidently. But funny that Herring woman didn't see him."

"Probably short-sighted," said the Colonel promptly. "She wears glasses and has that peering look. She'd see and recognize Mrs. Long because she was quite near, but if Stephan Varney was well away up the hill before she got to the window she might not see him. In any case, that path's got quite high walls on either side."

Mrs. Long was suddenly back, in a state bordering on hysterics.

"If you're thinking it was me it wasn't! I wouldn't kill! But he might, though he is such a nice young man. My— my husband was wicked in some ways; he got to know things about people. He told me that Mr. Varney was carrying on with someone and wouldn't want to have it known."

"Carrying on with someone?" Emily repeated incredulously. "In *Marshton?*"

"Yes, Mrs. Varney. Thomas said it would make a good stink if it was known, but that was all he told me." Mrs. Long seemed to try to pull herself together and her voice was suddenly almost cunning. "There are plenty of others who have secrets. And I know one in particular." Then she turned and departed again.

Emily, cold with shock and distaste, scribbled silently, and Mr. Pike suddenly jumped up and flung open the door.

"Mrs. Long? Is Betony down here? Will you ask her to come and see us, please?"

Mrs. Long rounded on him like a fury, every trace of meekness gone.

"You'll leave my child alone, Mr. Pike! Betony knows nothing at all and she's a sensitive girl and has been upset enough by this business of the flood and her father's death."

"Still, she came through the churchyard and we must just ask her one or two questions. I promise we won't upset her more than is necessary."

Mrs. Long seemed to recognize the voice of authority for Betony arrived within a minute or two. She looked very small and white and much more untidy than usual; small wonder after the night in the church. Under her arm she still clutched the volume of Yeats' poetry, and her diary poked up out of her pocket.

"Come in, Betony dear," said Emily gently. "We just want to ask you one or two things."

Betony stood with one foot resting against her other leg. Her stockings were stained and wrinkled and her hands were filthy. She kept looking at them uneasily, as though conscious that they should not be like that.

"Betony, you came to see Mrs. Varney last night. What time was that?"

Betony, looking down, mumbled:

"I—I don't know. It—it was late. I w-was late coming

home from school. It was getting dark."

"Well, why did you come?"

"B-because I w-wanted to b-borrow some books. Mrs. Varney had been k-kind, lending me b-books."

"How long did you stay?"

"Oh, only a very few minutes. Not m-more than five."

"And did you see anyone else either when you were arriving or leaving?"

Betony gulped.

"O-only Mr. Abel-Otty. He w-was coming through the g-gate just as I got to it. When I—when I was l-leaving, you know."

"Did you see which way he came? Down from the church or up from the marsh road?"

"I—no-o. He was opening the g-gate." Betony was so deathly white that Emily protested.

"She isn't well. Don't keep her long. What's the matter, Betony?"

"I—I had a pain. I'm all right, really, thank you, Mrs. Varney." But Betony looked more ghastly every moment.

"Well, just tell us exactly what you did *before* you reached the Vicarage," Mr. Pike said briskly, refusing to admit that the child's distress confused and upset him.

Betony gulped again.

"I w-was l-late coming from school, but I didn't w-want —I w-wasn't in a hurry to go home b-because of my father. H-he had been awful the night b-before. And I wanted the Yeats' poems. So I didn't go home when I got off the bus. I went up the path and through the churchyard"—she spoke very fast—"and down to the Vicarage. It was very d-dark and h-horrible and I w-wished I'd gone round by the road. The w-wind was awful, but the church looked b-beautiful. It always does."

"And you didn't see anyone?"

Betony broke into wild sobs.

"No. I didn't see *anyone!* And I'm going—I'm going to be sick!"

"Oh, do let her go! Betony, go and find your mother quickly. It's all right." Emily took her to the door, one arm round the shaking shoulders. "It's the shock and the wrong kind of food. You'll be all right soon."

When she turned back into the room her face was angry.

"Oh, must you do all this?"

"I think we must," said Mr. Pike firmly. He looked at his watch. "I asked your nephew to come at about—oh, here he is now!"

Stephan came in swiftly, bringing with him a breath of icy air. His overcoat was glistening with melting hail and he looked quite the most assured person who had entered the study so far.

"Well, here I am! First murderer, so it seems by the bits I've overheard and the looks I've been receiving. And it's going to be one hell of a day! God help those who are still stranded!"

Chapter 6
MORE SUSPECTS

AT THE sight and sound of Stephan Emily immediately felt much better. Of course the whole thing was rubbish; all that talk about "carrying on" with someone local. Stephan might have passed through the churchyard at the fatal time, but he had certainly had no cause to murder Thomas Long. Even if he had been rashly kissing a village girl it wasn't even faintly possible that he would do murder to keep the fact quiet, and, judging by what she knew of Stephan, she hardly thought him capable of the mild indiscretion of pursuing local girls. Stephan, she knew, numbered a few young women amongst his friends; he had nothing against women, but she was ready to swear that he gave them few thoughts.

Now he shut the door, and, swinging round a straight-backed chair, seated himself astride it and leaned his arms on the back. What light there was from the window fell on the darkening stubble on his chin.

The gaze he turned on Mr. Pike and the Colonel was alert and half-amused. He had fine eyes, clear and very intelligent, though the left one still bore a trace of redness, which was clearing up with every day that passed.

Mr. Pike removed his pipe, cleared his throat and consulted his chart, which was beginning to look decidedly intricate. The Colonel lit a cigar and looked at Stephan benevolently. He liked attractive, athletic young men and thought the fact of the delicate eye a great pity.

Stephan glanced in Emily's direction, gave her a reassuring grin and then looked back towards the two men. He made no attempt to break the silence.

"Well—er . . ." Mr. Pike plainly found Stephan a more difficult proposition than any of the previous people. "First murderer, eh? Well, I wouldn't go so far as to say that, but I must admit that you seem to be in a sticky position, young man."

Stephan looked at him with dislike.

"Just why? I'm a bit fogged about that."

"Now what time would you say that you arrived at the Roaring Bull yesterday evening?"

"Just on twenty-past six or thereabouts," said Stephan quietly. "Colonel Pashley came in very soon after me, if you remember?"

"Yes," said Mr. Pike, half to himself. "That High girl only just missed seeing you, too, eh, Colonel? You must have emerged from your gate at about the same time?"

"May have done," said the Colonel gruffly. "But the wind was hell going along to the pub. I had my head down and my eyes half-closed most of the time. Cold winds always make 'em water. But I was determined to get a breath of air before dark."

"Yes, well . . ." Mr. Pike made a tiny note. "Will you tell us just where you were before you arrived at the pub? Which way you came and where your walk took you and so on?"

Stephan's eyes were very bright and there was a hint of temper in his voice, but he answered levelly enough:

"I walked up the coast to about three miles beyond Blane;

then I turned inland and climbed up on to Blane Beacon. It's only about four hundred feet high, as you know, but it does give one a feeling of being up a bit in this flat country. Then I came back inland, along that old lane through the fields which cuts on to the main road about two miles from here. After that I came down the main road, through the churchyard and down Church Lane, intending to come straight back here. As I neared the gate I thought that I could do with a quick drink—it hadn't occurred to me before—so I went straight on down the lane and along the marsh road."

"Oh!" said Mr. Pike, somewhat deflated. He had been looking forward to confronting Stephan with the two people who said they had seen him entering, and possibly leaving, the churchyard. "I may tell you that I have one witness to prove that you entered the churchyard. At what time was this and how long did you linger?"

"Oh, about ten past six or thereabouts, I suppose," said Stephan, unmoved. "And you can see for yourself that I can't have lingered long. It wasn't the evening for loitering, especially in a churchyard."

"But you'd have long enough to sling a stone at someone you saw ahead. You must admit that?" said Mr. Pike smartly.

"We-ell . . ." Stephan cogitated. "Thomas Long was murdered, I gather, just near the south porch. Therefore he could hardly have been ahead of me as I walked across the north of the churchyard towards the top of Church Lane. There's apparently no proof that he was dragged about, or anything like that."

"No, he seems to have lain just where he was struck. But we have only your word for it that you *did* pass to the north. There are one or two small paths that cut across or up to the south porch."

"So there are, but I didn't take any of them. Nor did I see the slightest sign of the body nor of anyone else in the churchyard. It was as silent as the grave, I assure you, except for the noise of the wind. Of course there are plenty of highish tombs and monuments between the north path and the place where he was lying. I can't say that someone wasn't hiding there. But I didn't throw the stone, and I can't in fact—much as I regret it—help you at all." His tone expressed no regret whatsoever.

"A pity," said Mr. Pike, while Emily scribbled furiously. Stephan gave her a quick look, but made no protest.

"And as you went down Church Lane did you meet anyone?"

Stephan hesitated.

"Well, yes, I did, as a matter of fact. I met Mr. Abel-Otty just as I neared the bottom of the lane. We said 'Good evening,' and that was all. I supposed that he was going to the Vicarage and he was here when I got back. I wondered what he wanted at that hour on such an evening, but I didn't give it any more than a passing thought at the time."

"You saw Mr. Abel-Otty at what must have been a fraction after a quarter past six? Just where was he?"

Stephan thought for a moment.

"Well, I'd just passed the bit where the wall is high; you know, where there's that gate into the little timber-yard? There's a cottage on the other side—the Woodrows', I think."

"He was past the side windows of the Griefs' house?"

"Oh, yes. He was just nearing the Woodrows' cottage, I tell you. Does it matter?"

"Just checking up on everyone's position," said Mr. Pike smoothly. "Did you later see Miss High?"

"No, I don't think so," said Stephen, looking blank. "Should I have done?"

"She admits that you may not have seen her. She was just leaving her house; was, in fact, somewhere by the gate, but she says that you had your coat collar up and your head a trifle bent."

"He shouldn't have had," said Emily. "He's supposed to keep his head up as much as possible."

Mr. Pike ignored the interruption.

"Mr. Varney, does it strike you as strange that Miss High immediately went up Church Lane, walking very fast, and yet she didn't see Mr. Abel-Otty anywhere in front of her?"

Stephan seemed to be getting caught up a trifle in the fascinations of the problem.

"Well, she should have done," he said readily. "He was walking quite slowly—ambling, almost—and the lane goes almost dead straight up the hill. She'd surely have seen him in front of her, even though the light wasn't very good."

"She says she didn't, but perhaps she simply didn't look. Now, Mr. Varney, it seems to be my duty at the moment to ask personal questions—"

"I can't say that I agree with you, Mr. Pike."

"Well—er—the village people expect some kind of investigation and the fact that I and the Colonel here are carrying it out seems to be calming them. Mr. Varney, what was your quarrel with Mr. Long?"

Stephan's long, strong hands tightened suddenly on the back of the chair.

"My quarrel with him?"

"Yes. It seems to be common knowledge that you had a fierce quarrel with him, during which you said you'd kill him if he said the same thing again—whatever it was."

"One says that sort of thing. I naturally didn't mean it."

"Naturally. But what was the quarrel about?"

Over Stephan's face came an obstinate expression. He said stiffly:

"I hardly feel that it's your business. In fact, I think it's damned cheek on your part to—"

"No, hardly that," said the Colonel peaceably. "When the police get here—"

"When they do I might consider telling a responsible person, though it can have no bearing whatever on the case."

"It seems to give you a motive for murder." Mr. Pike was definitely enjoying himself, and Emily felt increasing distaste and horror. She would have liked to abandon her shorthand notes, and yet something kept her there. It might be as well to know exactly what was going on.

"I assure you that it was not. I don't go round irresponsibly putting people out of the way—even disgusting rats like Long."

"Mrs. Long avers that her husband told her that you were 'carrying on' with a local woman, and that it would have caused considerable trouble if the fact had come out."

Stephan leaped to his feet.

"Mr. Pike, you're a fool! And you can carry on your damned impertinent investigations without my further help. I was carrying on with nobody. Good God!"

"Then what was the quarrel about? It was evidently something that caught you on the raw."

"I'm easily caught on the raw just now," said Stephan darkly. "My temper's not what it was, as you'll soon be finding out. If it wasn't for this eye of mine—"

"Now, my boy!" The Colonel was on his feet.

"Stephan!" Emily could not stop herself.

But Stephan had gone, and Mr. Pike shrugged his tweed-clad shoulders. He managed to look neat and almost his usual self in spite of his experiences.

"There's more to that than meets the eye. We shall find out in the end. But it's suspicious—very suspicious indeed! He was in the churchyard about ten past six, and so far we've discovered no one else who was there earlier."

"The murder needn't have been committed until rather later, I suppose?" said Emily with a dry mouth.

"Well, not much later. Don't forget that Caroline High, who saw Stephan just turning on to the marsh road, was up there within five minutes, and unless we believe her guilty—" He paused. "It might, however, have been committed earlier. Mrs. Long might easily have been up there earlier, come down again and then, for some reason, thought she had better go back."

"But she looked into the pub about six and saw that her husband wasn't there."

"So she did. Well, it's still a mystery," Mr. Pike admitted

unwillingly. "Mr. Abel-Otty seems to be chief suspect just now. He went up the lane at a quarter past six and he arrived at the Vicarage at twenty to seven, according to Mrs. Varney. Where had he been in the meantime? Not picking daisies!" And he gave a short guffaw.

The same question was put to Mr. Abel-Otty himself when he appeared. He looked in an extremely bad temper, as well as cold and unshaven.

"This damn bloody flood! There's my wife in tears again, and me with indigestion because of getting the wrong food and not much of that. I can't think what the authorities are thinking about not to have got here by now."

Emily glanced at the window, beyond which was a blowing curtain of sleety rain. The screaming wind was driving it against the panes.

"No plane or helicopter could survive for long in this, and no boat either. But there were planes over very early, according to Mrs. Sainty. They'll come, Mr. Abel-Otty. Don't worry."

"Mr. Abel-Otty, what were you doing between six-fifteen, when you passed the side windows of the Griefs' house, and six-forty, when you opened the gate here?" Mr. Pike was just then only interested in the murder, and he had never had indigestion in his life.

Mr. Abel-Otty went red and began to bluster.

"Doing? Why, nothing. Never did pass the Griefs' blasted windows at six-fifteen. That old woman is a witch—or you can spell it with a 'b' if you like!—and so is her revolting daughter. All teeth and bad temper. It must have been much later than that. I walked straight up to the Vicarage here, and, as a matter of fact, I noticed the time as I entered the sitting-room. It was just about a minute after twenty to seven. So I must have left home at about twenty-five to. Goes without saying. And I've something better to think about just now. All my notes and my typewriter fifteen feet under that bloody flood water, and—"

"Yes, yes, it's very distressing." Mr. Pike could afford to be sympathetic. "But Mrs. Grief and Minnie swear that the time was six-fifteen and the fact that Mr. Stephan Varney passed you just past the shop at that time proves—"

Mr. Abel-Otty went so purple that Emily made an alarmed movement.

"Yes, of course I did meet him. But it proves nothing. Neither of us had our watches held out so that we could mark the exact time. I—"

"Stephan Varney arrived at the Roaring Bull at not quite twenty-past six, Mr. Abel-Otty. I was there myself and the Colonel arrived only a minute or so later."

Mr. Abel-Otty, still purple, made a noise that was almost a snort.

"The whole thing's rubbish—blasted rubbish! Why *should* I murder the fellow? I never went near the churchyard. I tell you I walked straight out of my house, across the road, up Church Lane and met that Betony child at the Vicarage gate. That's my last word." And he managed to look so bull-like and obstinate that even Mr. Pike prepared to give it up temporarily. He managed one last shot, however.

"Mr. Abel-Otty, this is a time when one can't mince words. Had Mr. Long—had he in fact threatened to go to your wife and tell her you were—er—amusing yourself with some of the village girls?"

Mr. Abel-Otty looked as though he might explode.

"The idea! Sir, you forget yourself. In another age I would have challenged you to a duel for making such a statement. My relationship with my wife is of the happiest, and—"

"Nevertheless—and no blame attached—you have been known to snatch a kiss here and there—"

"I really think you must be out of your mind, sir," said Mr. Abel-Otty, with devastating dignity. "I should not be in the least surprised, if you are making similar remarks to others, to find that *you* are the next to be murdered." He managed to make a very creditable exit.

"Poor man!" said Emily. The Colonel and even Mr. Pike looked uncomfortable.

"But it's certainly fishy!" said Mr. Pike, cheering up. "And remembering that his wife had all that money left to her by an uncle . . ." He shuffled his papers and made several entries on his chart. "Now," he looked at his watch, "we've got a few minutes to sort ourselves out. I asked your husband to be here at—"

"You asked Richard to come *here?*" Emily's voice was sharp.

"I asked him if he would be good enough to spare the time to come and give the Colonel and myself an account of exactly what happened last night. He expressed himself as very willing to do so, and I think—here he is!"

Chapter 7
THE NIGHTMARE MORNING

RICHARD VARNEY entered quietly.

"He looks old," Emily thought, and her heart and body yearned towards her husband. "When the flood's over—when all this is over—I shall get to know him better. I shall appreciate him more than I have ever done." But she knew that she would never appreciate him more than at that moment.

The Vicar was tired, cold, wet and decidedly dirty. His clothes were dusty and marked and his hands were red and raw-looking. His face and his hair shone with moisture, for he had just come down from the church through the downpour.

"He ought to be looking after his cold," Emily thought, but admitted to herself that it seemed much better in spite of everything.

Richard Varney moved to the fire and stood there, calm and quiet, but his face was drawn and troubled.

"If I can help you—"

"Would you please tell us again just what happened last night, Vicar?" said Mr. Pike.

"Well, let me see—I paid one or two sick calls before my final one on old Mrs. Gotts. She, poor soul, was glad of company, and I had some tea with her. Then I went up to the church. It was a bad evening, as you know, and I had a cold in my head, but I wanted to look up some facts in the church books. They're kept in a chest in the vestry. I didn't take particular note of the time, but it must have been about six when I got there. Certainly no earlier."

"And how did you get into the church?"

"I had the key of the vestry door and went in that way. The wind was by then very high and was making a considerable noise. I lit a lamp and one of the oil-stoves and was there reading until close on twenty to seven. Then I thought it was time I was going home, so I left the church—"

"By the vestry door?"

"No, by the south door. And when I was turning the corner I glanced slightly to the left and saw the body sprawled between two tombstones, just at the side of one of the little paths. I was horrified, naturally. I made a hasty examination and then walked quickly to the Vicarage, where I found Mr. Abel-Otty, my nephew and my wife waiting for me. Very shortly afterwards Mrs. Sainty arrived with news of the flood."

"Why did you leave the church by way of the south porch when, in fact, it would have been quicker and easier to leave by the vestry door?"

For the first time Richard Varney hesitated, but he said steadily:

"I'm afraid that is just one of those things that happen without thinking. There was still light enough to see my way up the church, and on the way I paused to set the parish magazines straight. They had somehow got rather tumbled."

"And you heard nothing while you were in the church?"

"Nothing but the wind. It would have been almost

impossible to hear anything else. And, as you know, the vestry is to the north of the chancel. As far as possible from the south porch."

Mr. Pike made an entry on his chart.

"Yes, well, thank you very much, Vicar. That seems clear enough. What time did you leave to make the sick calls yesterday afternoon?"

"It must have been about three. And I finished up at Mrs. Gotts around twenty to five, I think. One of the earlier calls was to a quite distant farm, and I walked there as it was no day for cycling."

"When you left home your wife was alone?"

"No, she wasn't alone. A—a mutual friend had arrived for lunch and I left them together."

"Ah, yes," said Mr. Pike thoughtfully, and Emily thought she sensed disappointment in his voice and could not imagine why.

Mr. Pike nodded and Richard Varney prepared to depart. Emily found herself yearning to be with him at all costs—longing for them to be alone and able to forget the horror. But it was not possible, and she watched the door close after her husband with only a faint and inaudible sigh.

The next moment she had a shock.

"It's only fair to tell you, Mrs. Varney," said Mr. Pike, with unusual and somehow ominous respect, "that Minnie Grief has another theory. But since your husband—well, I suppose—"

"What is it?"

"Well, the Griefs saw someone—a man—driving up Church Lane in the morning. They are naturally inquisitive, as you know, and they saw the Vicar leave about three, but the car was still there when Minnie looked up the lane some time later. She knew that Mrs. Sainty was out, and your nephew, too, and so—"

Emily rarely flushed, but she felt the hot, furious colour dyeing her pale face.

"That wretched, spiteful woman! Can't I be alone for half an hour with a man without Minnie Grief thinking I'm 'carrying on'?"

"Very distressing; very annoying, I admit. But that's the story she's unfortunately putting about. *Was* it only half an hour?"

Emily said coldly, while the Colonel stirred restlessly:

"Really, Mr. Pike! My visitor left at just about half past three to drive back to Norwich. Fancy Minnie Grief not noticing that."

"It seems that she and her mother were both very busy in the shop during the latter part of the afternoon and it was nearly a quarter to six before one of them looked up Church Lane and found the car gone. Unfortunately, just at the moment we have to take note of—"

"I think you must have taken leave of your senses." All Emily's latent dignity was in force, but she felt sick with disgust. "And Minnie Grief's theory is?"

"Well, that you—that you . . . Of course, you're rather an unusual type of Vicar's wife and—well, so smart and good-looking and with more money—well . . ." And even Mr. Pike came to a dead stop, bogged down in half-sentences. Emily remained stonily silent. "You see, all the rumours are getting to me at the moment, because they know I'm in charge of the invest—er—I'm investigating this unpleasant matter, and of course the Colonel here. Mrs. Long is apparently hinting that she knows something about you that you yourself wouldn't wish to have broadcast. Something that her husband told her about yesterday. I—I did not want to question her, thinking that perhaps—well . . ."

"Question her all you like," said Emily. "The theory is that, not satisfied with my husband, I enjoy myself with other men when I have the chance? And that Thomas Long had tried, or actually was, blackmailing me?"

"Oh, now, my dear lady! My dear Pike!" The Colonel was most unhappy.

"Something like that," said Mr. Pike. "Nonsense, of course. But can you prove that this visitor left yesterday at half past three?"

Emily thought of the proofs on which so much work had been done since the departure of her publisher, proofs that were at that moment safely locked in her slip of a study. For Mrs. Sainty had locked *that* door before the hordes had arrived.

"As a matter of fact I certainly could. I could prove without difficulty that I was very well and safely occupied between half-past three and a quarter past six or so. But I have no intention of doing so. And will you tell me how I could possibly have known that Thomas Long would be in the churchyard just then, conveniently placed for a large lump of flint to batter in his head?"

"You might have taken a walk and chanced—"

"A walk? On such a night?"

"Other people did—plenty of 'em," Mr. Pike pointed out.

"In fact, the churchyard seems to have been a positive attraction. I must do my duty, Mrs. Varney—"

"Then do it by having some sense," Emily retorted tartly, though she had a suspicion that she was being unfair to him. The circumstances were extraordinary and with so many vicious rumours flying around it was probably small wonder that the Vicar's wife should come in for her share of the suspicion.

Mr. Pike began to go over his chart, muttering to himself:

"Mr. Stephan Varney through the churchyard at ten past six. Seen to enter by Mrs. Long. Mrs. Long herself near and possibly in the churchyard shortly afterwards. Mr. Abel-Otty enters Church Lane at six-fifteen and then mysteriously disappears. Where *can* he have got to if not up into the churchyard?"

"Perhaps the Woodrows were looking out of their front windows and saw him," suggested the Colonel.

"That would be no help. We *know* he passed their cottage just then. Where did he go after that? There's something extremely fishy about it. In fact, you must admit it's the most damning circumstance of the lot. Ah, well, perhaps we'd better go up to the church and see how things are getting on. I believe in mingling with the people just now; some further facts may come out."

The rain was heavier than ever, but there seemed nothing to keep her at the Vicarage, especially when she heard that Richard had gone back to the church, so Emily seized a mackintosh from the stand in the hall, tied a plastic hood over her hair and plunged out after the men. At the gate they met a party of village youths, carrying a loaded and very wet tablecloth between them. In it was a wide assortment of tinned goods, which, it seemed, they had managed to salvage from the shop.

They were very wet, but triumphant, and certainly the meat and other food would be a great help in the urgent problem of feeding the stranded people. Mrs. Grief would groan that she was ruined, no doubt, though Emily had already done her best to reassure her over the question of compensation.

The rain and sleet were lashing over the tombstones and the scene was utterly desolate. Beyond the edge of the hill, dim in the gathering mist, could be seen the spreading flood waters. A few wet and depressed-looking cows were peering over the churchyard wall.

The wind was so violent that even the men were forced to cling to the tombstones when each gust threatened to throw them off their feet.

The scene within the church was not much more cheerful. More soaking-wet furniture had been brought in, and so had several more draggled and terrified-looking people. Emily comforted them as well as she could and sent them off to the Vicarage, assuring them of warmth and hot drinks. Then she followed Mr. Pike and Colonel Pashley down the nave, feeling obscurely that she should keep them under her eyes.

Betony was back in the church, sitting curled up in a pew, writing again in her diary. Her mother, who looked distraught and hardly sane, was talking loudly to a group of village women and Emily regarded her with disquiet. Mrs. Long had been dragging and spiritless for so long that the change in her was almost alarming.

Children were crying, dogs barking, and there was such a crescendo of noise and so many smells that Emily's head ached worse than ever. But she assured herself that no doubt others felt far worse. There was no sign of Richard, which somehow worried her more than ever.

Suddenly she saw Peter Love wandering along with something in his hand. He had a questing look. Mr. Pike stopped him genially.

"Now then, young man? How are you faring? Are you looking for someone?"

Emily drew nearer, with a sudden sense of foreboding. Peter was definitely holding a crumpled letter.

"I'm looking for the Vicar, sir," said Peter clearly above the noise. "I found this letter under a pew. Someone must have kicked it there. It's got no envelope, but I looked and saw that it belongs to the Vicar. 'Rev. Varney, Dear Sir.' I thought the Vicar might want it, sir. It's a letter from Mr. Long."

"From Mr. Long?" Mr. Pike fairly snatched the letter. "That's all right, my boy. I'll give it to the Vicar when I see him. You run along and find something to do. Read one of the books in the Children's Corner."

Peter looked justly incensed.

"They're only kids' stuff about Jesus, sir. I only read adventure books; space travel and things like that. And all my books are under the flood."

"Well, I'll buy you half a dozen new ones when the flood goes down and we can browse in a bookshop—see? You're a good boy."

Emily said quietly, as Peter went off:

"Mr. Pike, that letter belongs to my husband, and I think—"

"Yes," said the Colonel uneasily. "I really think, Pike—"

"I'm afraid all's fair where murder is concerned," said Mr. Pike and opened out the single sheet of paper. The writing was clear, bold and not uneducated.

The Rev. Varney.
Dear Sir,

I am taking up my pen once more in the hope that you will see fit to take notice of me. It would not be wise to ignore me. I'm an impatient man and I need money. The garage is a slow way of making it, especially in winter.

Best way will be if we have a meeting. Be in the church— the vestry will do—soon after six tomorrow evening, Thursday, when we can discuss the matter to our muttial benefit.

If you aren't there it will be the worse for you.

Yours truly,
Thomas Long.

Emily felt the strength ebbing slowly out of her body as she read the letter over Mr. Pike's raised arm, but one part of her observant mind noted with interest that the letter was clearly expressed and there was only one spelling mistake. Mutual was spelt 'muttial'.

"Oh, dear me! Well, I'm damned and blasted!" exploded the Colonel, looking unutterably concerned.

"There!" said Mr. Pike, with satisfaction. "Even reverend

sirs aren't free of blackmailers, evidently. I always thought it was fishy that he should stay so long in the church on such an evening, and with a cold, too. So he was waiting to see our friend!"

"Mr. Pike, you're insufferable!" said Emily. "I should mind your 'investigations' less if you could manage to hide your enjoyment. It must at least be evident to you that my husband did wait, until long after at least one person had seen the body."

"Oh, but that may only have been a blind," said Mr. Pike amiably. "He may have been hiding round the corner of the tower, ready to catch our friend. Mr. Long would come up from the main road, and just as he got his back turned, and was about to round the corner by the south porch, it would have been easy to let fly with the stone."

"What is it, Emily? Why are you looking like that?" It was Richard Varney himself. He put his hand on his wife's arm.

Emily looked at him, at first dumbly and then, thinking it better to get in first, managed to say:

"Peter Love found a letter, Richard, and Mr. Pike took it and read it. From Thomas Long to you."

"Oh, yes," said the Vicar, very evenly. "I realized that I had lost the letter. Well, Pike?"

"It's evidence against you, Vicar," said Mr. Pike, folding up the letter and putting it carefully in his pocketbook.

"I realize that, but I can only repeat, and shall repeat to the police, that I was in the church from six till twenty to seven and did not see Thomas Long until I discovered his body. I was, as a matter of fact, very surprised when he did not turn up, and I waited as long as I thought necessary. I left the church by the south porch in order to see if there was any sign of him, and came upon the poor chap dead."

Mr. Pike's eyes were a trifle avid.

"Might I ask, Vicar, if Thomas Long really had cause to blackmail you? I thought a parson's life was supposed to be blameless—ha! ha!"

"No, you may not ask," said Richard Varney shortly. "And now I must leave you to your investigations, for I see that there is some more furniture arriving."

Mr. Pike and Colonel Pashley retreated into the chancel, and Emily, on a sudden impulse, opened the door and went into the musty quiet of the vestry. Even the shrouded body of Thomas Long was better company than the milling, noisy crowds in the nave. She felt that she had had more than enough of the covert looks, the half-heard innuendoes and the silent suspicion.

She looked at her watch and saw with astonishment that it was not yet half past eleven.

The nightmare morning was only half over and heaven knew what would happen before that interminable day was finished.

Richard! The faint shadow between them was suddenly more real; more menacing. What had Richard done in the past?

"Nothing—nothing awful or shameful!" she said aloud. "I don't care what it was, but I've got to know. He's got to tell me. We must share it now or we'll never really understand each other."

She stood there in the chilly little room, looking out

through a Norman window at the rain-swept churchyard. A bare tree near the top of Church Lane was bent right over by the gale.

She was not a particularly religious person—not nearly so devout, she had often thought, as a Vicar's wife should be —but this was one moment when there was nothing to do but pray. And Emily Varney prayed with all her warm heart for her husband, for everyone caught up in that nightmare business, and for the solution to come and clear up the soul-destroying suspicion.

And almost immediately something became very clear to her. Two could investigate the circumstances surrounding the death of Thomas Long. Mr. Pike had got a certain amount of information and was probably already convinced that Richard had committed the murder in a moment of terror, wishing to keep his mysterious secret safe.

She, after all, had written detective stories for years; she was the daughter of a Scotland Yard man—and a famous one at that. It was just possible that by gentler questioning and understanding she might at least eliminate the suspects one by one. She felt suddenly that there was something they had all missed; something quite simple that, once realized, would make everything clear. It was somehow there at the back of her mind, but she could not put her finger on it.

At any rate, she would put her idea into practice and she would start with Caroline High. In some ways Caroline had softened since the previous night; she had shown faint signs of cleaving to the Vicar's wife.

Caroline High; Mr. Abel-Otty; Mrs. Long; Stephan; her

own husband; and the child, Betony. For Emily was still convinced that Betony had seen *something*, if only her father's dead body.

Strangely comforted and suddenly confident, she turned her back on the rounded window and stood for a moment contemplating the shrouded body of the man who had caused so much trouble. Then she went out once more into the church.

Chapter 8
EMILY VARNEY TURNS DETECTIVE

THE first thing to do was to find Caroline High, but, looking round the church, Emily could see no sign of her. That, however, was not surprising in such a close-packed gathering, and for five minutes or so she wandered about, apparently aimlessly, looking for the gleam of a red head.

Perhaps, then, Caroline had gone down to the Vicarage for a change of scene or maybe a cup of tea.

All the same Emily felt renewed disquiet; perhaps she should not have left Caroline alone in the throng for such a long time. Surrounded by suspicion and unfriendliness what might she not do? Wild visions of the girl finding the door of the tower open and throwing herself off the top, or of casting herself into the flood waters, raced through Emily's mind, but she told herself not to be a fool. Caroline might be unhappy and frightened, but surely she had too much of a hold on life for that? It was not at all certain, though, for Caroline really seemed to have left all laughter, warmth and happiness behind her in London during those two years when she had been away. That was judging by all that had been said. Emily had seen her only once or twice when she and Richard had first come to live at Marshton, for Caroline had rarely visited her mother. But she had never forgotten the first time she had seen her, for then it had seemed to her that Caroline was beautiful and alive.

The Colonel had spoken about the child who had gone bird-watching on the marshes and she had heard stories of concerts in the village hall, when the youthful Caroline had danced. She had been a good dancer, so it seemed, though now there was no suggestion of rhythm in her step.

Well, she would go down to the Vicarage again and try to find her there. Somehow Emily was unwilling to start with anyone else. Caroline had been the first suspect and it seemed somehow sensible to start with her.

She went out once more into the rain, which was not quite so heavy, though visibility was much worse and the seemingly tireless wind still blew. Somewhat to her surprise Emily immediately spied two figures striding round the churchyard. They were a man and a girl, but for a moment she did not recognize either. Then a particularly violent gust of wind blew the scarf from the girl's head and her red hair blew out brightly. At the same time she recognized Stephan's athletic body and the old raincoat that he wore.

Stephan and Caroline! Not talking—that would have been impossible in any case—but striding along in what seemed to be an oddly companionable way. Caroline wore gum-boots and was swishing unconcernedly through the wet grass.

They had their backs to her and for a few seconds Emily stood regarding them thoughtfully, her arm hooked through the railings of a particularly hideous tomb that she had always hated.

Stephan and Caroline! Well, it was good of Stephan to take pity on the girl and suggest walking. She knew without the slightest doubt that it must have been Stephan who suggested it; Caroline would never have gone one step towards another human being.

Well, they would probably not brave the weather for long and she could catch Caroline afterwards. She turned and fought against the wind down to the Vicarage, planning to collect a note-book and to make her own chart.

A little more order seemed in force at the Vicarage. The children were all sitting about drinking milk and most of their elders were indulging in yet another cup of tea. Mrs. Sainty appeared as if by magic and thrust a steaming cup into Emily's hand and she carried it upstairs, after acquiring the key of her study. How blessedly quiet it was in the little room, but bitterly cold! The electric fire was out of action, of course, and the wind was finding its way through every unsuspected crack in the window-frame.

She seated herself at her desk and sipped the tea thoughtfully. Then she drew out a large sheet of paper and began methodically to draw the churchyard and the surrounding paths. At the side she entered all the facts that she knew and ended by drawing minute little figures. *That,* so far, was clear; that was as much as Mr. Pike himself knew. Now the thing was to learn more about the movements and motives of the people concerned. It would take infinite tact, but Emily felt that she could do it. If only she could prove to her own satisfaction that most of the suspects were innocent it would at least be a real starting-point.

There was always a chance, of course, that the murderer had been someone totally unsuspected. The Colonel, for instance. Could he possibly have reached the churchyard and got back to the inn by six-twenty without anyone knowing? It seemed hardly likely, and, in any case, he had no apparent motive. It was not beyond the bounds of possibility that many people in the village had had cause to wish Thomas Long dead, but they had not, evidently, been near the churchyard at the fatal time.

No, all the evidence pointed to the people mainly concerned. But it was not Richard—it certainly could *not* be Richard! She did not want it to be Caroline High, and Mr. Abel-Otty was surely too sane and human . . .

There was no real profit in such thoughts and Emily folded up her chart, put it in her note-book and stowed both away in a deep pocket.

Start properly with Caroline High.

Warmed by the tea and a little more cheerful, she locked the study again and returned to the church. This time Stephan and Caroline were just coming through the kissing-gate through which the path from the main road passed.

They saw her and Stephan waved. Emily waited for them and Stephan shouted when they were near enough:

"We've been down to the edge of the flood—beastly! There's all sorts of flotsam and jetsam, but nothing useful within reach. We just had to have a blow!"

"I should think you got it!" Emily shouted back, her eyes on Caroline's face. The wind had whipped colour into her cheeks and she looked for the moment almost cheerful.

When they reached the south porch—Richard Varney had decided to lock the west door again as the wind seemed to find its way round to it so persistently—Emily said to Caroline:

"Would you come and talk to me for a moment? I—

there's something I want to say to you."

Caroline looked rather surprised, but she said quite willingly:

"Yes, of course, Mrs. Varney. But where can we go?"

"There's only the vestry, I'm afraid. But if you mind . . ."

Caroline shook her head.

"What's a body when so much is happening? Besides, I gather he's decently covered up."

"Oh, he is, and it really is quiet in there. The door's very thick and keeps out a lot of the noise."

The two women threaded their way across the church and up the north aisle. Caroline's hair was very wet, but she did not seem to mind. She ran her fingers through it to lift it and then shook her head violently, so that the drops flew.

"Phew!" she said, sounding more human than she had done since the terrible business started. "I feel better. Your —your nephew is kind, Mrs. Varney. He saw that I—it's awful having nothing to do, and—"

"Yes, Stephan's a good sort beneath his casual manner." said Emily quietly, shutting the vestry door and taking off her wet mackintosh.

Caroline gave one almost casual look at the silent figure in the far corner and then leaned on a high-backed chair.

"What was it that you wanted to ask me?" Her voice held no defiance, rather it sounded friendly and a shade curious.

"Well, I really wanted to talk to you. You see, it's awful keeping things to oneself and I know you can be trusted not to chatter. There isn't another woman who—"

Caroline looked at her quickly. Then she said suddenly

and surprisingly:

"You're worried stiff and you've got a headache. But your husband didn't do it. It's nonsense."

"Oh! You've heard that—"

"Peter Love told Stephan he'd found a letter that Thomas Long had written to your husband, and that Mr. Pike had taken it. Mrs. Varney, it's a beastly business, but I'm beginning to feel that there must be a solution somewhere. I swear to you that I didn't do it."

"Yes, and I didn't either," said Emily with a wry smile. "Oh, yes, I'm in it, too. Mr. Pike thinks I could easily have nipped up to the churchyard and thrown the stone, and apparently I had what he thinks is good reason. I had a secret that Mr. Long knew about, and his wife is hinting that she knows what it is."

Caroline looked at her gravely.

"Had you really a secret, and—and how did *he* get to know?"

"I have no idea how he got to know. It's a most mysterious thing. Yes, I have a secret—a silly and paltry one, and one I should certainly not do murder to keep, though I'd prefer that the villagers didn't learn it. That's just because it suits me personally, for various reasons. You've heard of A. E. Sebastian?"

Caroline looked astonished.

"Of course. Most people have. I think his books are marvellous, though I don't read murder stories as a rule. But—"

"Well, that's the secret—and keep it under your hat, just in case it doesn't have to come out. *I'm* A. E. Sebastian."

The colour in Caroline's cheeks had not faded and now her dull green eyes flashed into sudden life and interest.

"Mrs. Varney!"

"Yes, it's true. But it hardly seems suitable for a Vicar's wife to be a well-known novelist, so I don't tell people. I'm telling you now because it justifies me a little in what I'm going to do. I'm used to murder in fiction—thinking out problems and clues and time schemes and so on, and my father was Chief Commissioner at Scotland Yard before he died. It does seem to give me some qualifications, though I could wish that my brain felt less addled at the moment. You see, the moment I knew that Richard was really suspect I made up my mind to investigate this—this business myself. I feel as though I shall get further than Mr. Pike, who only puts people's backs up."

Caroline said simply and directly, with more warmth in her voice than Emily had ever heard there:

"Mrs. Varney, you love your husband very much, don't you?" Then, as Emily did not answer immediately, she added: "Oh, that was cheek of me! But I've seen you look at him, and I've always felt, in spite of what people said . . ." She floundered, embarrassed.

"Yes," said Emily. "I do love him. More than, at one time, I thought I could ever love anyone. I would do *anything* for him. I'll confess to this murder if he seems in the slightest real danger—no, that would be idiotic! What's the matter with me? But I want you to see—"

"I do see," said Caroline High. "You're telling me this because you want to try to make people tell *you* the truth and you're starting with me. I didn't murder Thomas Long,

Mrs. Varney, though there were times when I almost toyed with the idea. It was just as I said. I hated being alone in the house, and I did want to go into the church. Mr. Pike wouldn't have understood, but you—I know I don't often go to the services, but I love Marshton Church. I always have. When I was small I used to come in and sit on the steps of the font, and look at the blue light coming through the west window. I—I used to come here when I was very happy, and when I was miserable, too. And—and—lately I've often slipped in for a few minutes when I thought no one would be here. Not—not to pray. It's no good praying." For a moment her voice took on a hard note again. "No good at all. I prayed till I was sick at one time. But the shape of the church comforts me, and the smell and the feeling of oldness. And it's really beautiful. I think only Cley and Salthouse and Erpingham are more beautiful. And Cley is very like it, isn't it? With a faint blue light, and blue curtains round the pews, and the same tiles, and the wind blowing across the saltings."

There was a pause, which Emily did not break. Presently Caroline went on:

"So you see, last night when I felt desperate I thought I'd come up here just for a few minutes and see if it would make me feel saner and less lonely. I knew that it was never locked and I didn't think anyone would be about, but when I got near the south porch there was Mr. Long— dead. And I was horrified and thought at once that people would think I'd done it. Because I *had* cause to. He'd been blackmailing me for more than six months. I'd paid him all I could, and he said if I went away and got another job he'd tell everyone, including the Education Authority I went to work under, and—" She stopped abruptly, as though conscious that she had said too much now to draw back.

Emily said very quietly:

"Oh, Caroline, I wish you'd come to me. I might have helped. We might have done something together, and it was so bad for you to keep everything to yourself. I did want to be friends—"

"I knew that—from the first. But I felt that I didn't want anyone. Or only one person!" And Caroline's voice broke suddenly. She steadied herself with an effort. "I've told you so much I shall have to tell you the rest. It hasn't any real bearing on the murder—except, of course, that it'll make you see that I had cause to hate him."

"Tell me, then. What happened to you? You've been very badly hurt."

Caroline said quickly, and there was a hard note in her voice again, though her eyes were friendly:

"I always knew you were nice—and intelligent. How badly I needed an intelligent friend! But I was too proud. Now I haven't much pride left. You won't tell them unless you must?"

"I'll tell no one. If the police want to know later you shall do it yourself."

Caroline shivered.

"The police! I almost dread the floods going down. Oh, it was quite the usual sordid story. I—I was considered clever, you know, and I went to Oxford and afterwards I got a job teaching English in a London High School. I loved being in London, and I liked the school, on the whole. I had a little flat in Kensington, and I went to shows and concerts and it felt wonderful to be alive and to have some money of my own. Then I met—met Seumas. At a concert. We were introduced by friends, and—and I knew at once that I was going to like him awfully. In fact, it was love at first sight, though I never believed in it until then. I just couldn't think of anything else and he said he was the same. I think he was. It was perfect for several months. We did things together. Sometimes silly things, like walking and walking through the City when there was a full moon. I—I seemed soft and warm all through, and—oh, but you know, you know all that. We never mentioned marriage, but I just took it for granted and our friends did, too. They didn't know him well, but everyone admired him. He was in a symphony orchestra; he played the violin. He'd come from Ireland, from Dublin, when he was twenty-two. When I got to know him he was twenty-seven and I was not quite twenty-three.

"Then I—I knew that I was going to have a baby, and I—I told him. He was suddenly queer and far away and in the end he told me that he was married already, to a girl in Dublin. He hardly ever saw her. They had grown away from each other. But he went sometimes for a week or two and there was a child. She was a Catholic—I think he should have been, too—and she wouldn't divorce him. He—he said he'd do all he could, but after that he was different. He didn't want to see me nearly so often. And so I was proud and I tried to cut off from him and told him I didn't love him any more and didn't want him. I"—her voice shook badly— "I only did it because I could see that he was really tired of me and didn't want to be saddled with the child. I—I kept on at school for as long as I could, and then I had to give it up. I went to live in Sussex, and—and the baby was born there. Mother never knew. I used to get a friend to post my letters in London and to collect them from the flat, which I'd sub-let to someone I knew slightly."

She paused for so long that Emily, torn with pity for her, asked gently:

"And the child?"

"Oh, it was a girl—it had red hair," Caroline said rapidly. "It was really rather beautiful. But I had to go back to London and get another job, so I found a woman to look after it. She wasn't a bad sort and she loved Maureen, but she wasn't very intelligent. Very soon the—the baby caught diphtheria and died, and just then I heard that mother was ill, and the school here was vacant, so I came home."

"And Thomas Long?" asked Emily, feeling that sympathy was not wanted. "How did he know?"

"Oh, Mrs. Beech, the woman who looked after Maureen, found out where I lived, and it seemed she'd been rather fond of me and wanted to see me again. She had a daughter who lived in Norwich and she came here on the bus when she was staying with her. She got off by accident at the stop before the shop—by the inn—and she asked Thomas Long, who was standing there, where I lived. And somehow he got the whole thing out of her. She was rather a silly woman, and I think she thought everyone would know about the child. I'd told her I was a widow, and evidently she believed it. I nearly died when I found out what had happened. He guessed at once that I'd never been married at all. I—I—I was silly. I didn't even pretend properly. And—and I wished I could die, but I couldn't go away while my mother was alive, and, anyway, he said—"

"How that man deserved to die!" said Emily, so viciously that Caroline looked at her in surprise. She added more quietly: "Thank you for telling me. I think you should have done so before. It would have been better to share it with someone. And—and you're young. You will be happy again. Oh, not in the same way, but you will. You weren't made to be unhappy for ever."

Caroline retorted bitterly:

"I shall probably be hanged for murder."

"Don't be a fool! There isn't any evidence. The whole business is wrapped in mystery, and—"

"Well, if it isn't solved everyone will *think* I'm a murderess, which will be nearly as bad."

"As to that, they'll think I am, or Richard, or Mr. Abel-Otty, or two or three other people," said Emily sombrely, remembering with renewed fear that Richard had the clearest reason for having murdered Thomas Long. "No, it *will* be solved. It must be, for all our sakes."

After a little more talk they separated, Caroline, with commendable courage and imagination, to gather some of the children together for story-telling, and Emily to go in search of Stephan.

As she walked through the church she turned over in her mind the tragic story she had just heard. "We walked through the City when there was a full moon . . . I seemed soft and warm all through . . . It had red hair . . . It was really rather beautiful . . ."

Poor girl! No wonder she had looked hard and tight; too much happiness, pain and disillusion had been crammed into a short period.

"But she *will* be all right," Emily thought, side-stepping to avoid a sleeping terrier. "She had cause to murder him, perhaps, but I don't believe she did. I hope with all my heart that she didn't!"

Chapter 9
SOMEONE MISSING

EMILY found Stephan without difficulty. He was savagely stacking smaller articles of furniture.

"Oh, Stephan, I do wish you wouldn't!" she cried, immediately worried by something more everyday and practical. "I know it infuriates you, but do remember your eye. Do you want to go through all that again?"

Stephan faced her.

"Can't say I do. A more nightmare business than a detached retina I can't imagine. But I'm not bending—"

"You're moving much too violently. I wish you could find something more peaceful to do."

"Oh, well, give me the key of your study and I'll go and read. Will that be suitable recreation for a semi-invalid?"

"It would be much better. But the place is as cold as a tomb, and there's hardly an inch of room. It's only a cubbyhole and Mrs. Sainty has piled in all the valuables in the house, but you can go there if you like. I'll walk down with you. There seems nothing much that any of us can do, except endure until the floods go down."

"They've had another roll-call here and at the Vicarage. Most people are accounted for now, except for the people at Dyke Farm, and it's got a third storey, so they think they'll be all right."

"Well, thank God for that, anyhow. I suppose things might be worse. Where's Richard?" Emily felt as though she had asked that question a good many times.

"Gone down to help with salvaging more tinned food from the shop and from some of the other houses."

"In this terrible wind? I wish he wouldn't, but he won't be left out."

"He's the right stuff," said Stephan laconically.

They made their way through the churchyard, and Emily thought, as they battled their way through the gate and into Church Lane, that she would never again be able to walk those few hundred yards without remembering the horror and strangeness of those hours.

Once in the study she lingered.

"Stephan, I've decided to investigate this matter myself. Mr. Pike is only putting people's backs up."

"I should think he is. I can't tolerate that chap," said Stephan emphatically. "Jolly good idea if you step in. You've got the brain for it."

"I haven't just at the moment, but I don't feel it needs much brain, really. There's something we've all missed. I feel that strongly, but I can't put my finger on it. I feel as though I shall never be able to think clearly again. Stephan, tell me this once and for all—did you do it?"

Stephan looked at her with a flash of amusement.

"No, dear Aunt Emily, I did not. Not even to keep your fair name unsullied."

"What on earth are you talking about? What has my fair name got to do with it?"

"Quite a bit. That's what I quarrelled about."

Emily sat down in her swivel chair, which was placed before her typewriter.

"What? Because he was going to tell people that I'm A. E.

Sebastian?"

"Not on your life! He got on to that, did he?"

"Yes, he did. And I can't imagine how. But if you say that wasn't it—what *was* it? He surely didn't try to make you believe that I was 'carrying on' with heaven knows who?"

"He didn't try to make me believe it. He stated flatly that you were, and with—"

"Stephan, the man must have been mad! I've never 'carried on' with anyone but Richard. Was it just anyone? I suppose—"

"Not just with anyone, Emily dear. With *me*."

Emily gasped and then began to laugh.

"You're not serious?"

"Well, in one way I'm not, but *he* was. And I certainly wasn't going to spill the beans to that unutterable fool Pike. He informed me that he knew exactly why I was staying on for so long here at the Vicarage. What, he asked, were five years or so, when you were charming, so sophisticated, so good-looking? My eye was all eyewash, so to speak, and Richard must be blind, deaf and dumb not to see it."

Emily pushed back her hair in her characteristic gesture and looked at him more soberly.

"Oh, heavens! What a poisonous mind the man had! No wonder you were so furious with him. But I wish to goodness you hadn't said you'd murder him."

"So do I," said Stephan wryly. "But at the time I didn't think it funny at all, and I could have knocked him down then and there. You *are* charming, sophisticated—when you haven't got a dirty face and rumpled hair—*and* good-looking, Emily, but I know full well that you're otherwise engaged. If it hadn't been for that I might conceivably have considered—"

"And you might not," said Emily equably. "Well, I'm glad I understand, and it hardly seems grounds for murder."

"It wasn't. I cooled down pretty quickly, and saw the funny side of it. I certainly didn't nurse a bitter grudge and feel any urge whatever to sling that bit of flinty stone. But it does look bad. I was apparently the first to go through the churchyard at the fatal time—"

"You weren't, you know. Richard was through first. He got to the church about six."

Stephan lit a cigarette and said soberly:

"It's a bad do! I know he's amongst the suspects. I've caught no end of nasty remarks. What was the letter about exactly?"

"It just asked Richard to meet Mr. Long in the church soon after six o'clock, and said it would be the worse for him if he didn't turn up."

"But what had *Richard* to hide that Thomas Long might know of?"

Emily hesitated.

"I don't know. Nothing very much, probably."

"I'm jolly certain it wasn't. I'd trust Uncle Richard to the end of the world." Stephan was entirely sober.

Emily left him soon after that and was going slowly along the passage when she heard a giggle and a slight scuffle in one of the bedrooms. Thinking it was some of the children she opened the door a foot or two and was just in time to see Mr. Abel-Otty and the eldest Woodrow girl, Irene, spring guiltily apart. Mr. Abel-Otty coughed and straightened his jacket, and Irene, with a frightened look, dashed past Emily and away down the stairs.

It was a slightly embarrassing moment and Emily was in two minds whether to shut the door politely on him or to make non-committal conversation. Mr. Abel-Otty settled the matter by saying fervently:

"Thank God it was you, Mrs. Varney!"

"Why?" Emily moved slightly into the room, holding the door ajar behind her.

"Well, because you're human, even though you *are* a Vicar's wife, and you can hold your tongue." He was still rather red about the ears and Emily felt obscurely sorry for him, though she assured herself that she could hardly countenance kissing in the bedrooms of her own house.

"Thank you," she said dryly.

Mr. Abel-Otty groped for his pipe, produced it, and then made a gesture of frustration.

"No tobacco! Damn and blast! When will this flood go down? It's bad enough to be accused of murder without having to do without a pipe. And there's my wife raising hell still about the carpets and furniture. Got to have compensations . . . You do see that?"

Emily actually laughed. She really could not help it. He looked so guilty, embarrassed and defiant.

"Really, Mr. Abel-Otty, I don't know. I can't help thinking about the girl."

"Oh, she's all right. A few kisses can't hurt her, and she's got a job in Norwich—I expect you know that? She's going as soon as the flood goes down. Look here, do *you* think I murdered that bloody Long? Oh, pardon! No language for a

Vicarage, I suppose, but he *was* completely bloody!"

"We-ell, I hardly know what to think any more." Emily thought incredulously that it seemed very easy to get confessions out of people. It looked as though Mr. Abel-Otty were all set to tell her his story.

"Don't wonder at all. Everyone's gone crazy with suspicion. Hear that your husband's in it, too. The more the merrier, I suppose. They can't hang us all, *or* bring us up for trial. Some sensation that would cause! It would make law history, all right. But still I can't bear all the innuendoes that are flying about, and my wife—*she's* starting to ask where I was if I wasn't in the churchyard. And, as a matter of fact, she's the very last person I'd care to know. Look here, Mrs. Varney, they say confession's good for the soul and you *can* hold your tongue—"

"I suppose—" Emily began cautiously, but at that moment there was a sound of loud voices on the stairs and someone called frantically:

"Mrs. Varney! Mrs. Varney! Are you here? Oh, Mrs. Varney, do come quickly!"

Emily was out in the passage in a moment, everything forgotten but the fact that she was urgently needed. She rounded a corner, and there, at the top of the stairs, stood Mrs. Long, backed by a gesticulating group of village women.

"What's the matter?" Emily asked sharply.

"Oh, Mrs. Varney, have you seen Betony?"

"Betony?" Emily stopped short. It was certainly not what she had expected.

"Yes. We thought she might be with you."

"No. I haven't seen her for some time. Isn't she in the church or somewhere here?"

"No, she's not in the church, and she doesn't seem to be here. And we're so afraid . . ." Mrs. Long looked wilder than ever. "I'm so afraid something has happened to her!"

"What *could* have happened to her?" Emily asked, but her heart had once more leaped with fear. "She's too old and too sensible to go near the flood waters, and—"

"But there be evil people about!" wailed one of the women. "One murder and now—do she be murdered it'll kill 'er mother!"

"I'm quite sure that she hasn't been murdered," said Emily emphatically, and now all thought of Mr. Abel-Otty and his confidences had faded from her mind. She never even looked behind her to see if he was in sight. "She may have found some quiet corner somewhere. Have you been up in the attics? You know how fond she is of being alone and curling up with a book or her diary, and it was rather noisy in the church."

She soothed them all she could, but, after a quick search in the attics and in every likely corner in the house, she had to admit that it was mysterious to say the least.

The sleety rain was drenching down again and surely the child could be nowhere out of doors? Though she had repudiated the idea of a second murder, the thought was somewhere in Emily's mind as she dashed up the wet lane to the church, with the wind driving her on. She kept on seeing Betony in her mind's eye—the child's pale face, her equally pale hair and her clear-cut, intelligent face seemed etched in her memory. Betony crouching over the fire with her satchel on her back . . . Betony saying that she would like to find Yeats' Innisfree and keep cats there, a grey one and a ginger one . . . Betony's absorbed expression as she read the poem that began 'The host is riding from Knocknarea'. Was Betony never to find her way to that strange and rather haunted county of Sligo in Western Ireland and see the great, flat height of Knocknarea for herself, with the beautiful western bays not far away?

Emily knew suddenly that she was very fond of the child, had given her a little of her heart that day she had sat close to her amongst the sea lavender, with the summer wind breaking softly over them and the corn-gold uplands showing in the distance beyond Blane.

In the church there was pandemonium and Emily, looking round, could see none of the men who might have helped. Where was the Colonel, Mr. Pike, Dr. Love? Gone down to drive up two more cows who had swam, terrified, through the flood, she was told.

"She's not anywhere, Mrs. Varney!" shrilled someone.

"Didn't I be tellin' you? All murdered in our beds we'll be!" cried old Mrs. Gotts, who was still there and who seemed to have survived the discomforts of the past few hours better than most people. "Ah, the pore li'le girl! Mur—"

"Oh, shut up!" said Emily fiercely, and then, at the astonished look on the old woman's face, added hastily: "I'm sorry, Mrs. Gotts, but really it won't help if you blether on about murder. The child may be quite all right. What *could* happen to her with so many people about?"

"Well, where's she gone then? Tell me that!" said Mrs.

Long, almost shouting. "All I had left and—"

Emily pushed her way through the excited throng. "Has anyone looked in the tower?"

"Tower be locked," said someone. "Vicar has the key."

"No, Mr. Pike 'as it," said someone else. "Use it as a look-out they do."

The tower door was in a corner behind some of the piled furniture. Emily went there alone, since no one seemed to be interested. The door was shut, certainly, and might well be locked—should be, in fact. But when she put her hand on the old iron handle it turned and the door swung open.

She took a hasty look round. No one seemed to have noticed. They were gathered in noisy groups, talking about murder.

She slipped through and shut the door behind her. The winding stair was dark and the air smelt musty and icy cold. There was faint grey daylight from a lancet window round the corner, but the steps were worn and dangerous. Fortunately she still had her electric torch in her pocket from the previous night.

She switched it on and climbed rapidly. Could Betony possibly have found the door unlocked, and *why,* if she had, should she climb up those uninviting and rather terrifying stairs? To be alone, Emily told herself; Betony would like to be alone. But something told her that just then the child would be more likely to seek uncongenial company than climb by herself to the eerie, cobwebby twilight of the belfry and beyond.

Her heart thudded and she felt near-panic gripping her. "Fool!" she told herself, taking a hold on her fear. "She isn't here at all. But I'd like to *shoot* Mr. Pike for forgetting to lock the door."

She climbed so quickly that more than once she stumbled and had to clutch the ice-cold, flinty wall. She was in the belfry now and it certainly was no place for an imaginative child on such a day of violent wind. The tower almost seemed to rock in the gale. There was dust everywhere and the mouths of the bells had a horrid life of their own.

She went on climbing. She would just thrust her head out of the door that led to the roof, though Betony would not—*could* not be there.

The steps were now little more than a ladder, but she had a good head for heights, though just now her headache made her feel dazed and somehow short-sighted.

The door was closed. She pulled it a little. Fortunately it opened inwards and faced south, but she could hear the wind screaming louder than ever. The stones were soaking wet, and—

Emily froze where she stood, for she was not alone on the tower. There was someone crouching on the wet stones, peering over the battlemented edge. Someone with hands encased in worn woollen gloves on which the moisture sparkled.

"Betony!" Emily could not stop herself, and, in spite of the wind, the child heard. She swung round and, slipping from her half-crouching position, sprawled on the soaking stones within a foot of Emily's hand.

"My dearest child!" cried Emily and somehow drew her through the door. It was one of the worst moments of that nightmare morning.

Chapter 10
EMILY MAKES PROGRESS

EMILY got the child down as far as the belfry and then forced her into a sitting position on an old, upturned box. Betony was very wet and cold, but it was evident that the first need was to calm and comfort her.

The child had broken into wild sobs and her face was hidden in the wet navy-blue woollen gloves; gloves that had certainly seen better days. They were stained and worn.

"Oh, Mrs. Varney! Oh, Mrs. Varney!" she cried incoherently between her sobs.

"Betony!" Emily knelt down and forced the child's hands from her face. "Betony, don't be silly. You're all right and you'll make yourself ill if you cry like that. In a minute we've got to go down and tell everyone that you're safe—they're very worried—but you don't want them to know that you're upset, do you? We can say that you wanted a quiet place and were sitting on the stairs, after having a peep from the tower. But we *can't* say it if you go down with a streaky face and a cobweb on your ear." And she produced a fairly clean handkerchief and did her best to mop the pale, dirty cheeks.

Betony gulped and shook and suddenly clutched one of Emily's cold, roughened hands.

"Oh, Mrs. Varney! I'm so glad you came! I—I was so frightened!"

"What were you going to do?" Emily asked quietly,

though her heart still seemed to turn over at the memory of the child looking down over the parapet. Had she *really* intended to throw herself over the edge of the tower?

"I d-don't know. I truly d-don't know. But everything was so awful and—and I f-felt I couldn't bear it. And mother is so—so queer. It frightens me. She s-sometimes l-looks at me as though she doesn't really see me. I think it must all be a n-nightmare. Is it a nightmare, do you think, Mrs. Varney? W-will we all wake up?"

Emily was a great believer in saying things straight out, though the policy had never really worked with Richard; not with that hovering shadow. She said in the calmest possible voice:

"I don't think that things can be so bad that you really meant to throw yourself off the tower. Why, Betony, you'll look back on this day and remember that it was very terrible, but that it was worth living through it and putting it behind you for ever. Everything is rather dreadful, I agree, with so many people being suspected and everyone whispering and talking. And it's horrible being marooned on Church Hill. But it won't go on for long now. I heard someone say that the water's gone down a foot or two, and if the wind should drop things will soon be better and we can start clearing up some of the houses. There'll be a lot of work for everyone, you know."

Betony gave a little moan and then seemed to get a slight grip on herself.

"But it *is* like a nightmare, Mrs. Varney! I don't feel as though I'm me!"

"I don't feel as though I'm me, either," Emily agreed

ruefully. Then she fired at the child, though her voice was still gentle enough: "Betony, I want to know something. It matters very much to a good many people that we should hear the truth. When you went through the churchyard last night did you go near the church?"

Betony's face went whiter than ever and she clutched hard at Emily's hand. She mumbled something that sounded like, ". . . told a lot of l-lies!"

"Well, never mind. Tell me the truth now. *Did* you go near the church?"

Betony began to shiver, more, apparently, with nerves than with cold.

"I—I was going. I l-love the church. And I—I felt miserable and frightened and I thought it would c-comfort me. I d-didn't mean to be in there more than a minute before coming down to get the b-book from you."

"Oh!" Emily stared at her. This was the second person who had sought the centuries-old beauty and silence of Marshton Church when in trouble.

"But you didn't ever go in?"

Betony began to cry again. "No-o."

"What did you see, Betony? Did you see your father?"

With her head bent and tears streaming down into her quivering mouth, Betony nodded.

"I thought you did. It can't really be important, but I wanted to know. You ran away, I suppose? Well, but why didn't you tell people? Why didn't you tell me?"

Betony suddenly stopped crying again and looked full at Emily. Her eyes were huge.

"I—I couldn't at first and then I knew—I knew that I'd

been a coward. Perhaps he w-wasn't dead and if I'd done s-something—told someone—he wouldn't have died. I'm a m-murderer!" The word hung in the air of the belfry before the sound of the wind blotted it out.

Emily sat back on her heels, relief in her heart.

"My dear, good child! So that's what has been worrying and frightening you? By the time you saw him he certainly must have been dead. Why, it was after Miss High saw him. It wouldn't really have made the slightest difference whether you spoke or not, though I wish you'd told me. It isn't good to keep things to yourself, especially frightening things."

"No-o, Mrs. Varney." Betony rose suddenly to her feet. She looked, somehow, much older than her age. "I—I think I'd better go and f-find my mother."

"Yes, we'll go together. And you ought to go down to the Vicarage again and have a hot drink and sit by one of the fires."

She went down the stairs in front of Betony and quietly opened the door at the foot. The first person she saw as she looked out into the church was Mr. Pike, who, looking flustered, was advancing with a large iron key in his hand.

Emily dealt with him summarily and had the slight satisfaction of leaving him wordless, without a chance to offer apologies and explanations. Then she seized Betony gently by the arm and went in search of her mother. Their appearance was greeted with exclamations of relief, and the news went rapidly round the different groups. Betony would have been surrounded, but Emily kept the child close to her.

"She's quite all right. Mr. Pike left the tower unlocked and she was alone in the belfry. It got rather frightening up there as the wind's so strong, but she only needs a hot drink. Here's your mother, Betony. I want to speak to her for a moment, so perhaps Miss High will take you down to the Vicarage." She signalled to Caroline High, who immediately grasped the situation and marched the child off.

Emily looked uneasily at Mrs. Long. The woman really did look odd; her eyes were so wild and her untidy grey hair and dishevelled clothes made her seem rather witch-like. She drew her aside into a corner near the vestry door.

"Mrs. Long, forgive me for speaking plainly, but I think if we're not careful Betony will have a breakdown. She's gone through a lot since last night and these unsettled conditions are not good for her. You must keep this to yourself, but I think you ought to know that she might have flung herself off the tower."

Mrs. Long flinched, but she spoke in an unfriendly way.

"Betony's all right, Mrs. Varney. I wish folk would leave my child alone. It's that Mr. Pike who upset her."

"That and the fact that she *did* see her father's body in the churchyard last night and has been suffering from a troublesome conscience because she thought she might have saved him if she'd told people in time." Emily hesitated and then fired a shot in the dark. "Mrs. Long, what would you say if I told you that there are witnesses to prove that you *were* in the churchyard last night at the important time?"

The words did not have the desired effect. Mrs. Long

merely said sharply:

"I'd say they were telling a lie, but it doesn't surprise me. There's a great many people not telling the truth just now. I was not in the churchyard. I only went a bit up the lane, and that's Gospel truth."

It might be, and she had certainly not looked in any way taken aback, but Emily felt that in a strange way the woman was removed from what was happening around her.

Mrs. Long said viciously:

"Trying to put the blame on innocent people, that's what you're doing! You or that husband of yours. Maybe the pair of you are in it together. *You* had a secret to hide and so did he."

"Mrs. Long," said Emily, with dignity, "I had a secret, it's true, but I kept it simply because I did not think it any affair of the villagers. If your husband told you what it is then surely you can see that it wasn't a very important one? The thing that puzzles me is how he ever came to learn it."

"That's easy," said Mrs. Long sullenly. "There was a letter from your publisher in a book you lent to Betony. The child never saw it. Thomas picked up the book before she read it. Always mad, he was, when Betony had anything clever to read. And there it was, addressed to you, but it talked about your books and royalties and things, and there were some titles. Thomas always was inquisitive and he asked at the library. They told him they were by 'A. E. Sebastian' and even he'd heard of him—her, I mean." For a moment there was respect in Mrs. Long's voice. "He said you must have your reasons for not wanting people to know. Likely you'd put us all in your books and were afraid of libel. A great one for people's secrets, Thomas was."

"So that was how it was!" Emily was relieved to have another piece of the puzzle—however unhelpful it might be—fall into place. "Very careless of me, and I do seem to remember losing such a letter, but—"

"I haven't told anyone what the secret was yet," said Mrs. Long, even more sullenly. "But don't go murdering me to keep it dark."

"Really, Mrs. Long!" Emily gave the whole undignified and upsetting business up as a bad job. "Tell whom you please. And keep an eye on Betony."

"Wretched woman!" she said to herself, as Mrs. Long turned away, muttering. "Oh, dear! I do feel as though everyone's horrible. But I suppose it looks very bad to her. *If* she's so innocent herself. But somehow I feel more suspicious of her than of anyone else. And I'm damned uneasy about her, too!"

It was almost time for the improvised mid-day meal. People were going down to the Vicarage to get the tea jugs filled and others were coming up with tinned goods and anything else that was to hand. Dr. Love began to dole out milk to the children, talking to each one jovially as he did so.

Emily herself was suddenly conscious that she was desperately hungry and she made her way back to the Vicarage. In the porch, as she paused to shake her mackintosh, she encountered Mr. Abel-Otty. He had a mug of tea in one hand and a hunk of meat on a large crust in the other.

"Thought I'd come out here where it's quiet," he said. "Even if it's wet enough and cold enough to give one pneumonia. Don't know when you're going to get the smells out of your house, or out of the church either. Anyhow, the Vicar's cleared one of the outbuildings for the children to play in, and you're lucky to have a home at all."

Emily hesitated. She hardly felt like staying in the icy and rain-swept porch to talk to Mr. Abel-Otty, but it was as good an opportunity as she would get.

"Mr. Abel-Otty, you were going to tell me something earlier on."

Mr. Abel-Otty looked embarrassed,

"Using you as a confessional! That's not the function of a Vicar's wife, is it? But perhaps you'll tell me what you think? Suppose I'll have to tell the police eventually, if I don't want a noose round my neck, but I hardly feel like telling Pike and having my wife hearing all about it. It's a wonder it hasn't come out already. I told Irene to hold her tongue as long as she could, but you know what young girls are?"

"Yes, Mr. Abel-Otty, but what has it got to do with Irene Woodrow? Where were you between six-fifteen and twenty to seven last night?"

Mr. Abel-Otty gave a short crow of laughter, which he hastily stifled as several people carrying food and tea pushed past them.

"It's got everything to do with her. I was *with* her, see? Only I can't shout it all over the place before it's absolutely necessary, and perhaps the police will be able to hush it up. I couldn't have done the murder—unless I did it *before*

Mrs. Grief saw me going up the lane—because I was kissing sweet Irene and enjoying myself and so was she!"

"Oh!" Emily looked at him gravely, but there was a faint hint of laughter in her eyes. If this was true it was the first comparatively cheerful story that had emerged from the tragedy. Suddenly she remembered what she had entirely forgotten before, that when he had appeared at the Vicarage she had noted that he looked extremely pleased with himself. "More so than usual," she had told herself.

"That's a very awkward thing to have to explain," she remarked, after a pause.

"Isn't it?" said Mr. Abel-Otty fervently. "Bloody awkward, if you'll forgive me. My wife—well, she doesn't understand the pleasures of the senses, if you know what I mean. And Irene does. By Jove, yes! Though I assure you that there's been no more than kisses. They can go quite a long way, eh?" Then he seemed to realize that he was saying too much and added more soberly: "Well, there I was just passing the Woodrows' cottage and out comes Irene, looking as pretty as a picture. We just had a few words by the gate and then she said: 'Won't you come in for a minute? Mum's gone to the W.I. and I'm supposed to be going to see my girl friend, but it'll wait for a minute.' So in I went out of the wind and very nice it was, too. Except that I wasn't too happy in case any members of the family should arrive back sooner than expected. She'll back up what I say if she has to, though she won't like it, either. Mrs. Woodrow's rather a tartar and so is Woodrow *père*."

"Hum! Well, I should wait until the police come," Emily advised. "There's really no need to tell anyone else until then."

She left him soon afterwards and went in search of Mrs. Sainty and something to eat. Her thoughts were very busy. It would be easy to question Irene, but perhaps not so easy to find out if she were telling the truth. It was not beyond the bounds of possibility that the girl was really fond of Mr. Abel-Otty and might have agreed to shield him. Such things had happened before.

She found to her relief that Richard was in the kitchen, drinking tea and eating hunks of cold meat suspended on a fork. There were a great many other people milling about, but when Emily was provided for they retreated into a corner and seemed suddenly shut into a warm, secret world of their own. Though they had scarcely spoken a word Emily knew that her husband was glad to be with her. Some of the tight lines of worry disappeared from his face.

"If only we could be really alone he would tell me now," she thought, comforted. "At any rate, he'll tell me tonight." And there was no fear in her heart for what she might hear, only terror that Richard might be in danger of suspicion and even of conviction for murder.

"But there's no real evidence. Only the letter," she thought. "And that only proves that Mr. Long was going to meet him, *not* that Richard threw the stone."

At that moment there was a hubbub outside and a great many people thrust their way into the kitchen, making it almost impossible to move.

"They've come!" someone cried shrilly. "A boat's got through—a motor-boat! Quite a big one!"

"It's the Army!"

"No, it's the Navy!"

"They've brought food and medical supplies!"

"I must say they've taken their time. Thought they had a wonderful rescue service all ready, but other villages is worse hit where there isn't a hill, an' then the wind—"

"Mr. Pike's sendin' a message to the police, but *they'll* not get 'ere till tomorrow!"

Then the people had entirely gone, and Emily and Richard choked down the last of the meat and followed them out into the rain, up through the churchyard and down to the edge of the gathering crowd, close to the flood water.

"If they had long snouts and came from outer space people couldn't be more thrilled!" Stephan shouted in Emily's ear, as they kept their heads down against the wind.

The word most bandied to the rescuers was "murder".

Chapter 11
DEATH IN THE DARK

THE rescue party paid only a brief, dramatic visit. Once they heard that everyone was accounted for they were anxious to get away before the next high tide. The food and other supplies were unloaded, and, in their place, three old people and Sergeant Rust—whom Dr. Love was anxious to get to hospital—were put carefully on board.

Mr. Pike, with rain streaming down his red face, was much to the fore, and it was certain that the news of the Marshton murder would soon be all over Norfolk.

Nothing, the rescuers assured them, could be done before the floods went down a little, but the weather forecast was more promising and by morning—it was surprising how quickly these things happened—the main road might be clear enough to allow lorries through. The police would certainly be there without too much delay, but in other parts of the coast there was chaos and even for a murder . . . Well, they'd do their best, and if the wind grew less helicopters would bring more food and perhaps take off some more of the old people.

Everything felt very flat when the boat had gone again, but there was the business of carrying the supplies up to the church and Vicarage and the even more satisfying task of cutting up the loaves into thick sandwiches. Everyone was short of bread and the meal already eaten had filled no one.

For a little while, with the feeling that they were not,

after all, marooned forever on Church Hill with a murdered man and his killer, the tension abated a trifle, but before an hour had passed it was whipped up again—Emily did not quite know how. Once more rumours flew about. It was the Vicar; he had been hiding behind the church tower and had slung the stone . . . It was Stephan Varney, everyone knew that, because he had been heard to threaten Thomas Long . . . No, it was certainly Mr. Abel-Otty; he was a writer, wasn't he, and rather free with the village girls . . . Who best had reason to get rid of Mr. Long than his own wife? God knows, Colonel Pashley himself might not be innocent; after all, he'd been in the war, hadn't he, and was used to violence.

"That might apply to a great many people," said Emily tartly, hearing the last remark clearly.

The group of women backed away from her with blank faces, and she sensed rather than heard their "Likely it's the parson's wife. Mr. Pike says she's got no alibi."

It was only half past three, though by the way the time had dragged it could have been eight o'clock at night or later. The wind really seemed to be dropping and the rain had almost stopped. The sky, however, was dark and the flooded scene was very dim and misty. The air was still icy and fuel was going to be the next problem. There was not much oil left for the stoves in the church and the Vicarage stocks of coal and logs were getting low.

Everyone who was not still absorbed in gossip was bored and restless, particularly the better class people, who were not used to such discomforts and who, above all, hated to be herded together for so long. Mrs. Abel-Otty was inconsolable and would now speak to no one. Mrs. Love had joined Caroline High in desperately trying to find amusements for the children, and Mrs. Pashley was, with Mrs. Sainty, in charge of the stores. Those who had tasks at least had less time in which to think.

Stephan had long since abandoned all pretence of reading and finally he joined Caroline and Mrs. Love in organizing guessing games. There was little room indoors for much movement, even in the outhouse that had been cleared. There the smaller children were rolling and screaming and trying to fly paper aeroplanes.

Emily found plenty to do in trying to get the Vicarage and church into a better-organized and tidier condition. She felt tired to the bone, but she was better when she was doing something. Her investigations seemed to have come to a standstill, in much the same way as Mr. Pike's had, though she told herself that at least she had got a little further and to her the whole business was not quite such a fog of horror as it had been.

But Richard . . . If only she could speak to Richard alone!

The opportunity came just as she felt she could bear the uncertainty no longer. Richard himself sought her out in the dining-room at the Vicarage and said quietly but firmly:

"Emily darling, everywhere looks a thousand times better, but things won't stay like this for long. Tidiness is impossible when so many people are herded together. Have you got the key of your study?"

"Yes, Stephan gave it back to me. Do you want it?"

"Yes, and I want you. Come along."

Emily looked at him and then hastily looked away. She did not want the whole village to see her heart in her eyes.

They went upstairs together, Emily dragging at the stair-rail because her legs felt so heavy and tired.

Once they were alone she sent discretion and restraint to the winds and almost flung herself into his arms.

"Oh, Richard! Richard! I do need you so badly! I need you desperately!"

He held her very close, with his face against her tousled hair.

"Oh, my poor Emily! It has been bad, hasn't it? I need you desperately, too."

"You don't—often say so!" Emily felt like a young, love-sick girl, but she was past caring. What did dignity, sophistication, control, matter in private with Richard on this most nightmare day?

"No," said the Vicar slowly, "I know. I don't find it easy to say things like that. But the flood's loosened my tongue. Emily, there's one thing you must know—must be sure of. I love you with all my heart. And I didn't murder Thomas Long."

"I know you didn't," said Emily to his chest. She was tall, but Richard was much taller.

"Well, but most other people seem to think me first murderer, as Stephan calls it. And with some justification. Emily, that letter—"

"I guessed who it was from long before Peter Love picked it up in the church. I had one, too, a while ago, and last night when I was waiting for you I just suddenly knew that the letter you had had in the morning was from him."

"*You* had one? Why didn't you tell me?"

"I felt too disgusted. I wasn't scared about it and I didn't answer. He threatened to tell the whole of Marshton that I was A. E. Sebastian."

"Oh, as to that," said her husband, "there's no reason on earth why they shouldn't know. You do your duty as the Vicar's wife and what you do with your own time is nobody's business. And they'd be proud to know."

"Not now," said Emily.

"Even now, perhaps. Emily, I went to the church to meet Thomas Long because I hoped to talk some sense into him. I was going to do my best to show him the error of his ways, and if that failed—as I knew it well might in his state—I was going to the police. That's the truth."

"Of course it is," said Emily, waiting. She would not ask Richard for what he did not want to tell her, even in that strangely happy moment in the icy and overcrowded little room.

Richard Varney shifted her a little against him, but he made no attempt to finish their embrace. Rather he held her more tightly.

"Emily, I should have told you long ago. I'm ashamed that it's taken murder and a flood to get it out of me. I don't know what you've been thinking—what, for that matter, you've thought ever since we met. I have tried—sometimes I was on the point of telling you—but I *don't* talk about my deepest self easily. You do understand that? It's dead, lost, far in the past. But still I can't easily talk about it."

"Have you been married before?" Emily asked, in a voice that was much more tender than the ordinary words.

Richard Varney bent his head.

"No, but I nearly was. It—it was not long after I was ordained. When I was curate in a village in Lincolnshire. I met a girl—Emily, remember that I've loved only you since the moment I met you—but I was young then and deeply impressionable, I suppose. I never had the slightest idea that love could be like that. It possessed me utterly. It— there were times when it frightened and shocked me by its bitterness, though I was happy, too—unbelievably happy."

His voice was so difficult that Emily murmured incoherently. She did not dare to interrupt.

"She wasn't beautiful, really, but she seemed so to me. She was a queer creature, sometimes moody and sometimes gay, and not very often warm and loving in return, but it was enough to bind me to her more and more. I really felt that I should die without her, and so . . . You see, she was a Roman Catholic. She came of a family that had always been very devout; they wouldn't have been able to endure it if she'd married a Protestant, and, anyway, she wouldn't agree to marry me unless I changed my religion."

"Oh!" Emily saw clearly at last the terrible conflict. For she knew that her husband's faith meant a great deal to him; she knew that from his earliest youth he had always intended to enter the Church, that he had a real vocation. It was easy enough to understand the shame and bitterness and struggle and to visualize how deeply the realization that anything might conflict with his religion could have cut him.

"Yes, you know me well enough to be able to see something of what I went through. At last I made up my mind to become a Roman Catholic, and, of course, find another job. I felt as though my body and my senses were betraying me—in my darkest moments, that was—and yet it was my heart and mind, too. I really did love her. That was the damnable part of it, in a way. The other I might have overridden. I finally announced my decision. I wrote to the Bishop and our engagement was made public." Richard paused. "But before I could begin instruction Rachel had changed her mind. I never knew what happened. She never would explain. She was like that. She may not even have known. She got a job in London and went away almost at once and I never saw or heard from her again."

"Oh, Richard, *dear!*" There seemed no words of comfort for this early tragedy.

Richard Varney said, suddenly brisk:

"A very ordinary story, I'm afraid, and it's absurd, I suppose, to talk about broken hearts. But I never thought I would crawl out of that hell. The one thing was that I still had my faith and the Bishop was very understanding. He sent me to Melveney and I was there—first as Curate and then as Vicar—until I met you. Quite a number of years. The whole thing was hushed up and forgotten—or so I thought, until Thomas Long found out about it. I don't even know fully how he dug the story out, except that, by an unfortunate coincidence, his wife comes from the village where I lived at that time, and he visited it with her a few months ago."

"But, Richard, would it—would it actually have mattered so much if people had heard the story? Except that you hated to speak of it?" Emily faltered, shaken and yet curiously at rest. "After all—"

"Well, it would matter here, don't you think? The people here are very Low Church, and Thomas Long could have made a good story of my Roman Catholic leanings. But I was fully prepared to risk that. There never was, I swear, the slightest danger that I would have let him blackmail me."

"Of course you wouldn't," Emily said. "Oh, Richard, nothing will be so awful now that I understand. And the day *will* come when all this horror is behind us. Then—"

"Please God!" said Richard Varney. "But I don't like the look of things. And if this affair is never cleared up I can hardly stay in Marshton, with my parishioners muttering for the next twenty years that the Vicar got away with murder."

"Or his wife!" said Emily, with a slightly hysterical giggle. "Oh, they suspect me, too. Anyway, at the moment I feel I should be pleased to get away from Marshton. It can *never* be the same again."

"It could be. It could even be a better place without Thomas Long. The people are all right really, and on the whole they've taken this business of the flood with fortitude. When, after all, it's direst tragedy to them."

Soon after that they separated and Emily found that her feet no longer dragged. Neither did her ears struggle to catch each muttered word.

Darkness fell quickly, quicker that it had done on the previous evening. The rain had really stopped and the wind, while still bitterly cold, no longer blew at gale force.

The dangerous tide came and did no further damage, apparently, and by seven o'clock Dr. Love, armed with the strong electric lamp, reported that the water had gone down another two or three feet. The mist, however, had increased and Church Hill was being shrouded in a shifting, but gradually thickening, curtain.

In the church there was more order than there had been in the morning, but people were jaded and weary. Betony had been writing in her diary whenever Emily had looked at her, but in the end she, too, grew restless. She paced up and down the aisle not far from her mother.

Finally Emily, seeing this, suggested that she should go down to the Vicarage with her and borrow an absorbing story.

"Better for you than Yeats' poems just now. There're several stories that I liked when I was your age. Come along, Betony."

And Betony went, walking meekly beside the Vicar's wife, but not talking much. The children's books were up in Emily's study, but she took the child there unhesitatingly. Betony was in no state to be observant about galley-proofs and a filing cabinet.

At first the child was so stiff and silent that she thought she was wasting her time, but at last Betony relaxed a trifle and began to discuss the books. Emily told her what she remembered about them, they laughed over the old-fashioned illustrations, and gradually faint colour stole into the child's face. She began to look more normal than she had done for some time.

It was into this comparative peace that further tragedy

burst with stark suddenness.

At a wild commotion below Betony looked up to ask:

"Is it another rescue party, do you think, Mrs. Varney?"

"I don't know. You stay here." Emily rose, filled with a vague foreboding, and went out into the passage. The noise was much louder out there and it increased as she approached the stairs. She went down a few steps and, leaning over the stair-rail, called to the gesticulating and gabbling crowd below:

"What's the matter? What is it?"

Dr. Love disentangled himself from the crowd. He looked very concerned.

"Mr. Pike is lying just outside the gate here. He's been hit on the head with an iron bar. He's dead."

Chapter 12
IN THE MIST

FOR a moment Emily could not believe it. The frightened yet avid faces swam in a slight haze. She heard Dr. Love saying:

"It will be better if no one leaves the house for a while. No, please don't take that cocoa up to the church yet. Mrs. Varney, *you* come. You've got your head screwed on. I've sent for the Colonel; one or two sensible people had better see the body."

Emily pulled herself together with an effort. She had no intention of going to pieces in front of the village people.

"Wait one minute. I've got Betony upstairs. I'll just tell her to keep out of the way."

She flew upstairs again and along the passage, thanking heaven that at least the smaller children were tucked up and asleep. The horror had not yet fully penetrated, but she realized that they were going deeper than ever into the mire of fear and suspicion. This second murder might set a spark to panic that might spread and spread, and oh, God! Where was Richard?

She opened the door of the study and found Betony, with a rug round her shoulders, absorbed in a book. The child looked up, with only a mild, enquiring expression.

"Betony," said Emily quietly, "I have to go away for a while, but you stay here, and I should lock yourself in so that no one can disturb you. This is my private room and I don't want anyone else here. I'll try and come back later, but if you want to leave before then lock the door and bring me the key."

"Yes, Mrs. Varney," said Betony meekly, and then, sensing something in the other's rigidly controlled manner, she asked suddenly: "Has something dreadful happened? Something more?"

"Mr. Pike is—ill. I have to go and help."

The child would have to know soon, that was certain, but it was better that she should stay absorbed in her book for as long as possible. Emily went out and heard Betony lock the door behind her. The noise of voices was louder now, and a great many people were gathered in the hall, all, apparently, talking at once. Emily pushed her way through them with difficulty, trying not to hear the comments, trying not to realize the full import of this second murder.

Outside it seemed very quiet. The mist was wreathing about the garden and the wind had quite dropped. After the tumult the silence and stillness was infinitely uncanny.

The gate was open and there were lights beyond, and when she reached the spot there were Dr. Love and Colonel Pashley bending over the sprawled figure of Mr. Pike.

A few dimly seen and muttering people hovered in the background, folk who had come down from the church in time to witness the gruesome and, to some, fascinating scene. Dr. Love, never one to mince his words, swore at them fiercely, but they only retreated a foot or two, determined not to miss anything.

Emily asked:

"He really was murdered?"

"Oh, not a doubt of it. Someone must have come up behind him in the mist and whanged him one with that piece of iron." Dr. Love indicated a long thin iron bar that lay a short distance away. "It looks as though he was coming down from the church, and—"

"Oh, that's the bit of iron Richard put up this morning to support the part of the wall that the wind damaged," said Emily in a small, shaken voice.

"Yes. As a matter of fact I helped him to put it in place. The wall might have been a danger to people passing, especially to children. Someone decided it would be a good weapon and biffed him very neatly and with a good deal of strength. He seems to have gone down like a stone, only a minute or two before I found him. See! There's very little blood, so it looks as though our murderer is lucky again. Oh well, we'd better get him moved into the outhouse with the flood victims. This is a bad do!" And Dr. Love straightened himself and wiped his hands down his trousers.

"By Jove, a terrible business!" said the Colonel, who looked quite overcome. "This will mean further trouble and the people are in an unsettled state already. Give a lot for it not to have happened."

"We'll have a job to find out who did it, too, I bet. Of course it would happen at a time when quite a number of people were wandering about with food and cocoa. Suppertime—my God!" groaned Dr. Love, who was hungry and could have done with his own supper. "Damn this blasted mist—it's getting thicker! Pashley, we'll have to get a door or something and get the body out of the way. Can hardly leave him here until the police come. He makes the place look like the cover of a lurid thriller. It's clear enough what happened, anyhow. He must just have reached the gate. I must say the chap *asked* to be murdered, but still—"

"All the same, why *should* anyone murder him?" asked Emily, and her own mind answered her at once. "Because he had discovered something that was dangerous to the murderer. Something about the first murder."

Her mind seemed to be spinning round in circles. Where was everyone who might be implicated? Where was Caroline High, and Stephan, and Richard? Where, most of all, was Richard?

Dr. Love answered part of her unspoken question.

"That nephew of yours came down here just after me. Another couple of seconds and *he'd* have discovered the body. Made a nice mess of his wrist he has. I think he's with Mrs. Sainty in the kitchen. I said I hadn't time to deal with him just then, but I will in a minute."

"What's been happening to him?" Emily asked quickly, instantly worried on another score.

"Oh, it seems he tripped over a tombstone in the mist and he sprained his wrist trying to stop himself falling. He looked quite green, poor lad."

"Oh, but he mustn't fall. It's the last thing he must do. His eye—"

"I don't think he did fall. He managed to save himself, but at the cost of his wrist. But the body seemed more important to me just then. Look here, Colonel! I'll keep guard, if you go and see about some kind of stretcher."

Emily and the Colonel turned away together and the muttering group, now considerably supplemented, wavered and broke in the misty lane.

The Colonel said in Emily's ear as they went up the garden path:

"Bad business. Great shock to me when the news was brought to me. Dread what may happen now. Knew Pike was heading for trouble, but didn't think anyone would bash his skull in. I was down here having a cup of tea; suppose he may have been coming to look for me. Er—Mrs. Varney, should be glad if you'd keep your eyes and ears open. Got to find out what happened if we can and you're an intelligent woman. Hear you're out of it, thank God!"

"I suppose so. I was with Betony upstairs and had been for half an hour or so. Several people saw us go up. I'll do what I can," Emily said, but she felt too sick and dazed to feel that she would be much use.

"Come up to the church with me when we've moved this chap. May be needed. Good at stemming panic."

"Am I? I don't know." Emily paused in the porch, staring at his tall figure in the mist.

"More sense than most and the people like you. Oh yes, they do, in spite of the idiotic rumours that have been flying about all day. Now what am I to find to carry Pike's body on, do you think?"

Emily made a few suggestions, and then made her way to the kitchen, where she found Stephan in the midst of a milling crowd. He was having his wrist bandaged by Mrs. Sainty.

"What a fool thing to do!" he was saying bitterly. "I didn't half give it a jab, but my one thought was not to jerk my damned eye. Then I came on down the lane and there was

Love bending over the body. It gave me quite a turn."

"Why were you coming down here?" Mrs. Sainty asked sympathetically.

"Why? To get some tea or cocoa or something and I was coming too fast in the mist. Thanks, Sainty dear, that'll be fine."

Mrs. Sainty had a soft spot for Stephan Varney and she said soothingly:

"It's given you a shaking up. Fright, I expect, in case you damaged your eye. Just you sit down in this chair by the fire and don't move, and I'll make you a nice bed here later. No going up to the church again for you, even if the Vicarage *is* supposed to be reserved for the aged and the mothers of young children."

"You can't say I'm either," said Stephan. He complied meekly, though the gaze he turned on Emily was faintly amused. The amusement changed to concern, however, when he saw her face.

"Hullo, Aunt Emily! It's a bad business about Pike, but the chap really was asking for it. Never thought anyone would, though."

"No." Emily was conscious that silence had fallen and she had no desire to discuss the matter before some of the sharpest-tongued old gossips in the village. "Are you all right, Stephan?"

"Oh, I'm quite O.K. now that Mrs. Sainty is coddling me. But I seem destined to be a crock."

"A bit of coddling won't hurt you. I'm going up to the church with the Colonel." Emily lowered her voice. She was standing very close to Stephan. "Do you know where

Richard is?"

"I suppose he's up at the church. I'm afraid I don't really know. I haven't seen him for some time."

Mrs. Sainty thrust a cup of tea into her hand and Emily drank it quickly, feeling the hot liquid helping to clear her brain. She would need every scrap of intelligence and endurance she possessed, she could see, so it was just as well.

Then she went out the back way and found the Colonel and Dr. Love just locking up the outhouse again. Dr. Love went in to see Stephan and Emily and the Colonel went out into the lane and walked rapidly up to the church. There was not a soul about—almost certainly the news of the murder had penetrated to the "church people" and they were prudently staying indoors. Probably fear had spread to such an extent that no one would dare to venture out alone, or even in groups, while there was what must now be assumed to be a ruthless murderer abroad.

It was very eerie in the lane and Emily jumped when something large loomed up just in front of her. But it was only a cow, apparently depressed, for it gave a dreary moo. The torches they carried only served to emphasize the mist, which was thicker than ever at the highest point of the churchyard. No sounds whatever came through it.

They paused for a moment and Emily shivered, more with fear than with cold.

"Oh, Colonel Pashley, will we *ever* get to the other side of all this?"

"Oh, yes, m'dear. Everything passes, as you're wise enough to know," said the Colonel comfortably. "But must admit that this is a bad patch. My God! That poor chap's wife! What were Love and I thinking about? We never so much as gave her a thought. This terrible business must have pushed the human element, so to speak, out of our minds."

Emily herself was shocked to find that she had not given Mrs. Pike one thought. She was, in any case, rather the type of woman whom everyone was inclined to ignore and forget; a pale, quiet, dull soul, incapable of anything but the mildest of pointless chatter.

"I'm dreading going in!" she said, and was conscious that her stomach felt as though it did not belong to her. Richard ... Caroline ... Mr. Abel-Otty ... Where were they? How were they taking this fresh blow? She found herself praying wildly, as the Colonel's hand fell on the iron door-handle, that everyone who mattered had an alibi. Especially Richard. Oh, most especially Richard!

After the misty darkness the church seemed very bright, though as usual the great beams of the roof and the tops of the higher arches were in deep shadow. There was, surprisingly, very little noise. In fact, everyone seemed to be held in a tension, a stillness. People gathered in tight little groups all turned to look at Colonel Pashley and Emily as they entered and shut the door behind them.

Emily's heart seemed to leap up and then swish down again, for Richard was standing on the steps of the font and seemed to have been addressing the pale, agitated-looking throng. He looked very pale himself, old and haggard, but he was there.

Colonel Pashley pulled at his collar and advanced slowly,

looking old himself, and deeply upset and embarrassed.

"A bad business, Vicar! Most distressing and—er—distressing." Colonel Pashley looked round until his eyes alighted on Mrs. Pike, who was sitting on a chair not far from the font, with a group of women round her. She looked white and shrunken, but a bright shawl that someone had draped round her gave her a garish air. "Needn't tell you, Mrs. Pike, how deeply I—er—regret it."

Mrs. Pike moved her mouth, but no sound came, and the women gathered closer round her, as though protectively.

Richard Varney said clearly:

"Colonel Pashley, I think it will be as well if you try to make things a little clearer. We have heard only various, perhaps garbled, accounts from people who saw the body and heard the talk at the Vicarage."

The Colonel pulled his collar again.

"Er—well, 'fraid Pike was murdered without a doubt. He must have been intending to enter the Vicarage, perhaps in search of me. I was having a cup of tea in the kitchen. Someone was evidently following him pretty closely—the mist does deaden sound—and just as he was turning in at the gate he was hit with a piece of iron that had been used to support a wall. Most of you probably noticed it during the day. Killed instantly, poor chap. Dr. Love, fortunately, was the one who found him, with Mr. Stephan Varney a close second. We've—er—moved him now, but it will be as well if people only venture forth in groups of two or three or more. After all, never know, and seems to me we should have made that rule before. Easy, though, to shut the stable door after the horse has gone."

Meanwhile, Emily was leaning against a smooth, cold pillar, trying to take in the scene. Her eyes anxiously raked the crowd, and after a moment she discovered Caroline High perched on the back of a pew. For a moment of astonished awareness she thought that Caroline looked both beautiful and happy, and then she told herself that it must have been a trick of the light, for the girl was still pale and dishevelled and her face was quite grave, even anxious. Mr. Abel-Otty was with his wife and Mrs. Pashley and his face was ashen, as though the shock of the news had been almost too much for him.

"What we've got to find out," said the Colonel, "is what Mr. Pike was doing before he left the church and who went out immediately after him. But—"

"Us never saw 'im leave!" shrilled old Mrs. Gotts. "Never saw nothin', us didn't. People comin' an' goin', and the murderer amongst 'em, most like. An' I never 'ad me cocoa."

"Oh, I think some fresh is being made. Someone will come up with it," said Emily automatically.

"Do we be murdered we may as well 'ave our cocoa first, that's what I say!" croaked the old woman.

"No one else is going to be murdered!" said the Colonel testily.

Mrs. Gotts gave him a knowing look and mumbled something about having heard that before.

The Colonel cleared his throat and did not attempt to argue.

"I thought you were a sensible woman, Mrs. Gotts. And you shall have your cocoa soon—by Jove, yes! We really all need something stronger than that, eh? But no can do. Now, let's get this clear. Did no one see Mr. Pike leave the church?"

There was at once a babel of comment, from which emerged the apparently true fact that a good many people were coming and going just then and Mr. Pike must have slipped out unobserved. One woman said he had been "messing about amongst the furniture" when she had last seen him, but she hadn't noticed him go.

"Well, we'll have to find and question all the people who left the church, if we can," said the Colonel, not very hopefully.

"Mr. Abel-Otty come in not long before Mr. Woodrow comes up an' tells us about the murder!" cried a voice, and Mr. Abel-Otty said on a high note:

"I'd been down to the Vicarage to get a jug of cocoa for our supper. As a matter of fact, when I was coming back I passed Pike in the lane—thought it was him, anyhow, but I didn't speak. The mist was thick and just then I tripped over a stone and nearly lost all the cocoa. I was hurrying, because of trying to keep it hot. And—I didn't take much note of this at the time—but there *was* someone not far behind him. I didn't really give it any attention; as a matter of fact I'd started to think about my new book—the one I'm working on now—and I was miles away thinking how I'd work in the flood and rush it through the Press quickly."

"Was it a man or a woman?" asked Colonel Pashley sharply, more interested in anything Mr. Abel-Otty might have seen than in his new work. "Surely you can tell us that?"

Mr. Abel-Otty looked vague.

"I wish I could say, but I can't. There just was someone in a dark coat or mackintosh. But it was nearing the top of the lane, where it widens out for a few yards. I really never gave it a thought, and, as a matter of fact, I passed a few other people as I cut across the churchyard. When I get thinking about my book—" Suddenly he drew out a handkerchief and mopped his brow. He looked ghastly.

A queer muttering started and Emily was conscious of the surge of emotion that went through the crowd. Mr. Abel-Otty was conscious of it, too.

"That's the truth, I tell you. I couldn't bash anyone over the head clutching a jug of cocoa and my wife and Mrs. Pashley will bear me out when I say that it was still quite hot when I got it here. And I certainly wasn't the only one who was out. Ask people. All I know is that *I* didn't murder him."

"Vicar was out!" cried a woman from the back pew, where she sat with quite a big child asleep in her arms.

Richard Varney said swiftly:

"Yes, I was out, and I'm afraid I was quite alone. It was so stuffy in here, and the night has turned so still and so much warmer in spite of the mist. I went down to the edge of the flood and I was there for some time thinking my own thoughts. I didn't return until the news had reached the church. So I'm in it, too, Abel-Otty."

"They was all out!" said Mrs. Woodrow, a normally silent and taciturn woman. "With my own eyes I saw Miss High coming in just before my husband. 'Er face was red an' 'er eyes bright an' she looked kind of excited."

Caroline High had started and her eyes sought Emily's. But she made no movement.

"I wanted air, too," she said very quietly. "I was just walking round the churchyard and for a while I stood in the north porch. I never went near the Vicarage."

"Did anyone see you? Did you meet anyone?" asked the Colonel, anxious to clear the girl as much as possible.

Caroline was very flushed again, and there was a defiant note in her voice.

"I don't know. I was just in the churchyard. I didn't murder Mr. Pike."

Colonel Pashley said suddenly, his keen eyes searching the crowd:

"Where was Mrs. Long?"

Mrs. Long was sitting huddled in a shadowy seat in the north aisle. In the dim light she looked more witch-like than ever and her voice when she answered was more shrill than usual.

"I was here! I never went out!"

"Can anyone back that up?" asked the Colonel. There was a silence, then a woman said:

"I dunno, but I think she was there all the time. She's been that queer earlier on; wandering about; now 'ere now there. But I think I could swear she was 'ere when Mr. Woodrow come in to tell us."

"I seen 'er comin' out of the toilets, but I can't remember just when," said another voice.

"I was right here. I never set a foot out in the mist. I suffer from my chest, as everyone knows," said Mrs. Long, in a stronger voice. "And what I want to know is, where's my child?"

"Safe at the Vicarage," said Emily promptly. "She was with me when the news of the murder came. I'll bring her up to you presently."

Soon after that the tide of speculation and suspicion swelled up and people huddled into closer groups. Colonel Pashley said to Emily:

"My God! Worse business than I thought! Why the *hell* couldn't the people who seem to matter stay together?"

"Because they didn't think, I suppose," said Emily, who felt that she could easily be sick there and then.

Richard Varney came up to them and for a moment his hand sought Emily's.

"Don't worry, my dear. Fool that I was to take a walk on my own, but I've had no time for thinking all day and it was peaceful down by the edge of the water. The flood's going down rapidly, by the way. The police should be here by tomorrow."

"The police!" said Emily faintly.

"It'll be better to get it into good hands. We're all too close to events to see them clearly. That's at least part of the trouble. We've got to get at the truth now."

"By Jove, yes," agreed the Colonel. "Can't live in the dark with two murders unexplained. Never know a moment's peace."

Emily had been forcing her tired, frightened mind to think.

"What about Dr. Love? Could he—is it possible . . . ?"

Colonel Pashley looked startled.

"The Doc's all right, surely? He *did* find the body, but *he* can have no reason for bumping off poor Pike. Know the chap was upsetting people, but still—couldn't help that. Difficult to change our natures."

"Well, Dr. Love did have the opportunity, but he had an alibi for the first murder and no apparent motive. That is, did anyone ever question the people at the farm where he—"

"Pike asked them what time he left and it tallied with the length of time he'd take to reach his surgery. In fact, he must have had to step on it. No, I feel that Love—"

"Well, look at it from another angle," said Emily, still forcing on her numbed brain. How had she ever thought herself good at seeing similar problems clearly? Fiction seemed to have no meeting-place with real life. "Where did the murderer go? He or she must have hit Mr. Pike and then very quickly disappeared, after laying down the iron bar. The fact that Dr. Love made no mention of hearing it fall shows that it must have been put down quietly, surely? It would have been fatal to walk into the Vicarage, though we must try to find out who did arrive just before Dr. Love. Dr. Love seemed to think that Mr. Pike had only been dead a matter of a minute or two when he found him. The murderer can hardly have turned and walked calmly back up the lane, or the doctor would have noticed."

"Hid in the mist," said the Colonel laconically.

"Yes. It was very dark just below the Vicarage gate and no one would have any reason to walk down there. I should think that the murderer must have gone down the lane a little, and then perhaps climbed the wall—there is a low place—and gone back to the churchyard by way of the field. Anyone at all agile could easily climb back into the churchyard and then slip quietly into the church. No one would notice, probably, unless there was a lot of blood, and there shouldn't have been. In any case, whoever it was could have taken off their coat as they entered and rolled it up. No one would have thought anything about that. Ought we to look at—"

"Everyone is wearing clothes belonging to everyone else," remarked Richard Varney. "You might try that, though. Here's mine, for instance, and this, as it happens, really is my own." And he displayed an old raincoat, stained, it was true, but not with blood.

"All the same there *wasn't* much blood," Emily went on, thoughtfully. "I wish I could think it had, but it might not have got on to the murderer at all. That was quite a long iron bar."

"It's probably too rough to carry finger-prints, by the way," said the Colonel. "But we've locked it up in the outhouse just in case."

The three of them were standing a little apart, near the west door, and suddenly the Colonel turned and spied Peter Love hovering near.

"What do you want, young man? We're busy just now."

"I know, sir," said Peter, unabashed. "But I thought you'd like to know. I didn't want to bellow it all over the place, but I know what Mr. Pike was doing before he left and I heard what he said."

He had all their attention at once.

Chapter 13
WHAT DID MR. PIKE KNOW?

THE Colonel, Richard Varney and Emily stared at Peter for fully half a minute before any of them spoke, and then Emily said quietly:

"Really, Peter, you do seem to get involved in this. You'd better tell us what you know."

Peter's eyes were bright with triumph and a suspicion of over-excitement.

"I'm going to be a detective when I grow up. I thought I was going to be a doctor, but my father says it's nothing but blasted forms nowadays and I call murder jolly thrilling. But I wish everyone wouldn't get into such a panic. I don't like that."

"Well, what did you *see?* Let's have it quickly," said the Colonel.

Peter said earnestly:

"I was jolly well bored stiff and I was just nosing about with my hands in my pockets, thinking. I wasn't taking much notice of anyone until I came all up amongst the furniture and I managed to knock one of the top chairs off and Mr. Pike was a bit narked. He was standing by that writing-desk that someone fished out of the flood—the one that has all the books piled on top. He was standing there with his back to me, looking at some of the books. Just sort of idly, as though he wasn't really thinking what he was doing. *I* wasn't thinking much either," said Peter, rather apologetically. "I just propped myself up against that nearest pillar, and I took out my knife—it's a jolly good one!—and began to whittle a little bit of stick I had with me. Then all of a sudden Mr. Pike sort of slammed round, and some of the books went sliding on to the floor. I heard him say: 'My God! Why didn't I think of that! But if she saw anything there's only one person she'd shield!' And then he almost cannoned into me and said, 'Have you seen the Colonel about anywhere, young fellow?' I said I hadn't, so he went straight out of the church by the south door."

"And did anyone else see or hear?" Emily asked sharply.

"No one could have heard," said Peter positively. "There was all the usual row going on. They could have seen, I s'pose, if they'd been interested. Seen him looking at the books, I mean, and then dashing off. He went off like steam, as though he couldn't wait a minute."

"And did anyone follow him? That's very, very important, Peter."

" 'Fraid I don't know. One of the smaller chaps beckoned to me just then, and I went to show him how to use my knife. It's so jolly boring for everyone," said Peter candidly, "being cooped up here. Next thing I knew Mr. Woodrow was saying that old—I mean Mr.—Pike was dead."

"And the books? Which book was Mr. Pike looking at?" asked Richard Varney.

Peter shook his head regretfully.

"I don't know, sir. After—when I'd heard about the murder—I did go and turn them over. They're mostly jolly wet, sir. I couldn't see anything that might give him the solution to the murder. But he seemed to think he'd got it. Jolly pleased, he looked; as though everything was clear as daylight."

"And you didn't tell anyone what you'd seen and heard?" A pause. "You didn't tell your father?"

Peter looked surprised.

"No, I didn't tell a soul, word of honour. I just turned it over in my mind and thought it must be jolly nice to be a detective. Then everyone started talking at once and getting no end upset and excited, and the Vicar here tried to calm them."

"Where was your father when Mr. Pike was turning over the books?"

But Peter looked vague and innocent.

"I don't know, sir. Surely you don't think he'd murder anyone, because I'm ready to swear he jolly well wouldn't. He's all over the place, you know. People keep on telling him their symptoms and he has to do what he can. I'm jolly certain now that *I'm* not being a doctor—"

"Well, you're certainly quite an observant boy. Now don't tell anyone at all what you've told us. Run along and—er—isn't it time you got some sleep? It's getting late," suggested the Colonel.

Peter looked at the watch he had been wearing so proudly since his last birthday.

"It's only nine o'clock, sir. I don't go to bed till half past and the pew I slept on last night was hel—er—jolly hard. I hope you catch the murderer, sir, but—but do you think it will turn out to be someone we *know?*"

"I'm afraid so," said the Colonel heavily, and they stood and watched the boy go off, ambling thoughtfully through the crowd.

"So Pike thought he'd got it!" said the Colonel. "And he

did get it, by Jove! Though not in the way he thought, poor fellow!"

"Someone else must have been watching and realized that he'd guessed," said Emily slowly. "It would have been easy enough to slip out after him and shadow him down the lane. But what can he have seen amongst all those wet and battered books to give him the slightest help?"

"We'd better go and see," said the Colonel. "Might suggest something to us as well, though if the murderer had any sense he or she will have removed it by now."

Richard Varney excused himself, but Emily accompanied the Colonel across the church to the piled and pathetic furniture. Some of it was now very high, and all sorts of incongruous objects were scattered about: opened and un-opened jars of jam, a dish of butter, one gum-boot, a broken pottery vase and a pail with a hole in it. The books were scattered on the top of the largish writing-desk that someone had salvaged from the flood waters. They were an uninteresting lot—a couple of lurid, paper-backed novels, the bad print nearly obliterated by sea-water, a French textbook, a cookery book, a pile of technical magazines, and several battered novels in strong bindings. There were a few others on the floor, but there was nothing that seemed to give the slightest clue to the working of Mr. Pike's mind and they were forced to give it up, baffled.

"There must have been *something!*" said the Colonel, annoyed. He slammed down one of the lurid novelettes, the cover of which depicted a luscious-looking blonde ogling a man reflected in an ornate mirror.

"Perhaps it was nothing to do with the books," suggested

Emily. "Perhaps he was merely looking at them absent-mindedly and an idea—the solution—suddenly came to him." Suddenly, to her alarm, everything went wavering and rather dim, and the Colonel put his hand on her arm, saying quickly:

"Look here, dear lady! You're worn out and worried about that husband of yours, though I assure you there's no need. No one in their senses will ever think him a murderer."

"I know," said Emily, ashamed to find her voice shaking badly. "But I wish with all my heart that he hadn't been alone in the mist when—when the second murder happened."

"Well, he certainly wasn't the only one. Fate seems to have conspired to get the lot of them out of doors just at the fatal time. There was young Stephan following in the procession, and Mr. Abel-Otty coming up the lane, if what he says is true, and Miss High—God damn it, I wish we could clear that girl!—wandering about on her own. And Mrs. Long really seems to have been one of the few lucky ones, though no one can actually swear that she wasn't out. You'd think people would be only too anxious to stay together under the circumstances."

"The trouble is that they've been herded together all day," said Emily.

"Well, we'd better get a bit of sleep, if we can, and bring our minds to bear on it in the morning. There'll be plenty to do tomorrow, in any case, if the water goes down and we can get at some of the houses. I was in Salthouse after the big flood there and the houses were feet deep in mud and slime."

"I'd like to go to bed, but I must talk to a few people first. I can't just slip away without doing anything." And Emily made a gallant effort to override her tiredness and depression. It must be awful for Caroline High. She could not leave the girl for the night, alone amongst hostile people, without a few words of friendship and comfort. It was good to know that at least she would not now be repulsed. If they all lived to look back on this time of flood and sudden death her friendship with Caroline would be one of the good things that had grown out of the horror. That and her warmer, safer happiness with Richard, now that the nameless shadow had gone.

Caroline was sitting on the chancel steps, a trifle removed from the general movement and conversation. Emily did not blame her, for during her passage through the church she heard many disturbing comments and part-comments. There was no calmness now in Marshton's huge and beautiful church. It seethed with speculation, suspicion, mounting fear. Murder! Murder! Murder! No one, it seemed, could think of anything else.

All the same, Emily was relieved and a trifle surprised to see that Caroline did not look unduly upset. She was sitting easily, with her hands loosely clasped round her knees, her head slightly bent, so that her hair slid forward over her ears and cheeks. She started when Emily came up to her, and then scrambled to her feet.

"Oh, Mrs. Varney! Isn't it appalling? I feel sure we shall all wake up. I—I just can't grasp it properly."

"I can't grasp it, either," said Emily tersely. "The only thing that is clear is that the people I care most about are still implicated. Oh, if only Richard had stayed in the church! If only *you* had!"

"I was only in the churchyard. I didn't go near the lane." Caroline spoke almost mildly. There was no trace of the hysterical girl of the previous night.

"But, my dear girl, you can't prove it. I wish to heaven you could. I don't blame you for getting some air, but couldn't you have gone with someone . . . ?"

Caroline did not answer for a moment. When she did she had changed the subject.

"Mrs. Varney, you're simply dead and you've had a headache all day."

Emily suddenly spoke, almost involuntarily.

"Do you know—I've been thinking—you are the first person I've told. Not even Mrs. Sainty has guessed, and she's usually pretty quick. Perhaps it's not very tactful of me to tell you, but somehow I'd like you to know. I think I'm going to have a baby."

Caroline looked at her gravely.

"Do you know, it had occurred to me to wonder. Shall you—shall you be glad?"

Emily said "Yes" almost brusquely, but in spite of her tiredness and worry a part of her heart was singing. A baby —Richard's baby!—of course she was glad. How could she be otherwise, whatever happened?

"I should try and get some sleep. You've been on all day."

Emily passed her hand over her hair.

"I shall very soon. And I don't think I can leave you here. I—I hate the atmosphere."

"So do I—both kinds!" said Caroline fervently. "I—I don't

like the idea of spending the night here, either, but where can I go? The Vicarage is reserved for old people and for—"

"Well, there's my little study upstairs. It's cold and there's hardly any room, but we might find you a few cushions and a blanket. Would it be better than the church?"

Caroline's relieved face rewarded her, and she went on quickly:

"Stephan's sleeping in the kitchen tonight. He hurt his wrist when he tripped in the churchyard and Mrs. Sainty is insisting on coddling him a bit."

Caroline said quietly:

"Yes, so I heard. I—I hope it isn't very bad?"

"No, I don't really think so, but it shook him badly. He was afraid for his eye. Well, be ready to come with me. I'll go and find Richard."

She found her husband in the vestry, struggling into his surplice. He turned a tired face towards her.

"I thought it would be a good idea to have a prayer and one or two well-known hymns before everyone settles down. It may help to calm people and give them comfort. Then I'll come, Emily."

Emily and Caroline stood together near the back of the church as the short service took its course. The singing was unaccompanied and very wavering, but the Lord's Prayer swelled up quite clearly, as though the people of Marshton really felt the need for help. For a few minutes the church was more itself—a little of the silence and peace came back, in spite of the litter and the smells.

It was during the short service that Emily noticed that Betony was back. She was standing by her mother, so white and pinched-looking that she might hardly have been alive. Emily's heart smote her, and as soon as she could she went up to the child.

"Who brought you back, Betony?"

"Dr. Love, Mrs. Varney. I asked him to. I—I locked up your room, and here's the key." Betony spoke in a very low voice.

"Thank you, dear. I'm sorry I had to leave you so quickly. You see—"

"I know that Mr. Pike was murdered," said Betony on a frightened note. "I know. I—I can't bear it! I wish—"

"It's terrible, but there's no need for you to worry. Try to get some sleep and tomorrow things may look better."

Emily hoped so fervently, but in her heart she believed that the nightmare would go on until it reached its appointed conclusion.

Five minutes later she, Richard and Caroline walked down to the Vicarage through the mist. All was fairly quiet when they reached the house and they went straight upstairs. Emily went with Caroline and succeeded in making the girl a nest that should not be too uncomfortable, though it was rather cramped.

As she turned to leave Caroline suddenly put up her arms and drew Emily against her. For a moment her lips brushed Emily's cheek.

"Thank you for being so kind and understanding. I—should have gone crazy this morning if it hadn't been for you. I—I wish I hadn't been so stiff and unfriendly for so long."

"Well, we're friends now," said Emily warmly. "Try not

to worry. In the morning—"

"In the morning!" Caroline repeated sombrely, withdrawing herself. "Well, we don't know what will happen. Good night, Mrs. Varney." She hesitated, as though about to say something more, then apparently thought better of it.

Emily found Richard just crawling into bed and hastened to join him. As the darkness engulfed them she breathed:

"Oh, Richard, this day seems to have lasted for ever! And tomorrow we shall have strangers all over the place. The police will be questioning and investigating, and, do you know, I keep on feeling that it's so simple, really. I feel that one side of my mind knows something important and yet I just can't quite get it. Whatever it is just escapes me. But I don't really mind anything so long as we're all right."

Her husband gathered her warmly against him.

"We're all right. As you say, it's the shining light in this maze of fear and suspicion. Now go to sleep, my dear. You're worn out."

Emily wondered whether to tell him about the baby, but decided that she would wait a little, until they could see the future more clearly. Richard was soon breathing deeply, but Emily found that, as on the previous night, her mind could not settle to rest. Now, in fact, there was more to disturb it. It seemed almost unbelievable that never again would Mr. Pike make entries on his chart and ask unwelcome questions. She had not liked him, but it seemed an abrupt and unnecessary end for one who had really enjoyed life a good deal in his own way.

Caroline High . . . Emily was puzzled about Caroline.

There had been a softness about her tonight that was not entirely explained by the fact that she had shared her hurtful secret. In fact, Caroline still stood in a most difficult position. And yet she had sat calmly and in almost a relaxed way on the chancel steps, with her red hair catching a gleam from the dim lamps.

Passionately Emily wanted Caroline to get clear of the horror and learn to live again; learn to be warm again, as she was meant to be. She wanted Mr. Abel-Otty, poor man, to be free of his troubles, and . . .

But always she was brought back to the awful question of two murders. The chances were, she supposed, that both murders had been committed by the same person, and what little evidence there was seemed to point to that recurring little group of people. *Not* Richard; not, surely, Stephan. But in the eyes of the village people they were very much included amongst the suspects. Mr. Abel-Otty, Caroline High, Mrs. Long, even Dr. Love. Dr. Love might not have had the chance to commit the first murder, but he had very certainly been in a good position to commit the next. But why? There seemed no reason at all.

Mrs. Long? But no one could even say that she had been out of the church, and there was no evidence that she had actually gone up to the churchyard on the previous evening, though she could have done, following Stephan. Only then, surely, Stephan would have seen Thomas Long just in front of him?

"If Mr. Pike could see it surely I can?" she thought, humiliated, but no solution occurred to her and she drifted into restless sleep at last. She awoke once or twice in the night, but each time she turned over and slept again. The last time she awoke it was almost light and she told herself that she must get up, but once again she drifted off, this time into a nightmare in which Caroline was in the dock accused of the double murder. She could see the girl standing there above the crowded court, white of face and still, with sunlight on her hair, and she felt herself gripped by helpless despair.

It was an infinite relief to be jerked back to the comforting appearance of Mrs. Sainty with a tray.

"Seven o'clock and a fine morning!" said Mrs. Sainty, quite as though there had not been two murders and the whole of Church Hill was wrapped in suspicion. "The sky's clearing and the flood's going down rapidly. Parts of the main road are clear, so I'm told, and a helicopter's brought food, thanks be!"

She thrust steaming cups of tea into Emily's and Richard's outstretched hands.

"In fact, all would be right with the world if it wasn't for the people in it. If I hear any more of this nasty suspicion and accusation I shall commit murder myself, and I know who'll be first to go. Mrs. Grief! That woman ought to be in her grave, where she could bother no one. And her daughter Minnie needs a man, though I don't often so far forget myself as to mention such a thing. Now drink your tea and don't worry. Everything's as nearly in hand as it can be."

"The flood's unloosened her tongue!" said Emily, giggling weakly, and she took a great gulp of tea and nearly choked.

Chapter 14
EMILY KNOWS

EMILY found it harder than ever to face the day that had dawned so grey and still. The fury of the gale and the lashing water seemed as though it had never been, and from the windows of the Vicarage it was easy to realize that the floods were indeed going down rapidly. Where there had been nothing but water below Church Hill there were now patches of gleaming mud and occasional squares of grass. Broken walls were coming into view and the houses no longer resembled arks—they looked now what they were, derelict and broken dwellings from which the water was retreating. It would certainly be some time before people could reach the houses on the marsh, for the mud and slime would for a while make almost as great a barrier as the deep, swirling water had done. But at least people would be able to get out a little and would not have to spend the whole day between the church and the Vicarage.

Emily leaned from an upper window and felt the air soft and almost warm on her face. There was a feeling of spring in it, even though there was no hint of sunlight.

Oh, if only, she thought, it was merely the receding floods with which they had to contend! If only there were not two unexplained murders and a thick curtain of suspicion! She shrank inexpressibly from the arrival of the police and the resulting investigations. What could they find, in any case? The only actual evidence was the two bodies and the weapons that had killed them, unless you counted Caroline High's pencil and the letter Richard had dropped. There was nothing else that was tangible; not even a preserved footprint in the churchyard.

Caroline High, emerging from the study, looked as though she had slept well. There was colour in her cheeks and her feet did not drag, as they had done on the previous morning.

"What's going on downstairs?" she asked, handing Emily the key of the room.

"Breakfast, I suppose," said Emily, without enthusiasm. Her whole soul yearned for coffee and thin toast enjoyed in peace and comfort, but she told herself sternly that she was not the only one who shrank from the general conditions. It must be far worse for Mrs. Abel-Otty and Mrs. Pashley, Mrs. Pike and Mrs. Love, who had nowhere to go but the corner they had made for themselves in the church. Still, no doubt today they would be able to make arrangements to go to friends or a hotel somewhere inland, until they could see what might be done about their ruined homes.

Today!

"Face it! Get on with it!" Emily ordered herself, and she followed Caroline down into the seething life of the hall and kitchen passage. The "church people" were coming in and out with jugs and plates, and the "Vicarage people" were sitting about in the downstairs rooms, talking endlessly and eating what food was available.

The eyes that followed Caroline and the Vicar's wife were curious, speculating, infinitely disquieting. Mrs. Grief was mumbling to her neighbour like an old witch. It was still

"Murder! Murder!" Emily felt sick, but told herself that it was inevitable.

Stephan was in the kitchen, marshalling the queue for tea. He, at least, seemed oblivious of the looks and comments and he was moving people along with cheerful, slightly double-edged comments that brought faint smiles to a few faces. His hand and wrist were bound up and fastened in a sling, but he did not seem to be in pain.

Emily wriggled her way to his side.

"How did you sleep? You look quite disgustingly cheerful, let me tell you!"

Stephan gazed at her quizzically.

"My good woman, it's an act. The truth is that I don't know how the first murderer *should* behave, so I'm clowning just to give them something to think about."

"Don't be a fool! You're *not* first murderer."

Stephan said more soberly:

"Go on. I'm first favourite in the eyes of about a quarter of the village. They'll be laying bets on us next; shouldn't be surprised if they've started already. Mark you, I sprained my wrist battering Mr. Pike on the head. Then I hid in the mist until Dr. Love had discovered the body and whereupon judged it safe to appear, with my tale of tripping over a tombstone. Believe me, I know it all. My God! What a life!" He dexterously picked up two empty cups with his left hand and thrust them at Emily.

"I'll allow you to break the queue—you and Miss High. Good morning!" and his eyes sought Caroline's. She returned his greeting composedly, and he went on: "After all, you've both got plenty of work to do. I'm told that the kids up at the church are going absolutely wild. Affected by the general atmosphere, I suppose."

"We're neither of us in any hurry to go up to the church, even if there *is* plenty to do," Emily said in a low voice, but she allowed Mrs. Sainty to pour her out a cup of strong tea and accepted a thick slice of bread and marmalade, though she had no appetite.

When she, Caroline and Stephan made their way up to the church through the still grey air, breakfast was more or less drawing to a close. The west and south doors were wide open, but even so the atmosphere was bad and Emily made a mental note that gallons of disinfectant would be one of the first requirements.

A rather deadly silence fell as they entered and all eyes were on them. A big lout gave a guffaw of ribald laughter, somewhat hastily stifled, and Stephan murmured:

"Enter the three witches! My God! It's a role that teaches one something, but I'm not yet clear just what. Where the hell's Uncle Richard? Someone say something!"

The tension broke almost at once and people got on with the business of removing the empty jugs and clearing up in a desultory and disinterested way. The talk was all low-voiced and uneasy; only the young people were noisy—in fact, they were thoroughly out of hand. Emily was just about to drive them out of doors, for though the grass was soaking wet they would be better in the air, when a startling diversion was caused.

A young, plump girl suddenly broke away from a group in the south aisle. Her face was scarlet and her voice shrill, and her words drew everyone's attention to her at once.

"I think you're all hateful, that I do! I don't know who the murderer is, but it isn't Mr. Abel-Otty. Slow, aren't you, the lot of you? Where do you *think* he was that first time, when old Mrs. Peeping Tom Grief saw him pass her window at six-fifteen . . . ?"

Emily took in the situation at a glance. She saw the arrested, avid faces. She saw Mrs. Pashley staring blankly, Mrs. Pike obviously not listening at all, Mrs. Love, kindly and intelligent, looking concerned, Mrs. Abel-Otty—she could not see her, but she must be somewhere in the church.

Mr. Abel-Otty was, however, very much to the fore. He appeared close to Irene Woodrow's side, red-faced and alarmed, his empty pipe clutched in one slightly hairy hand.

"Now, now, Irene! No one thinks I'm a murderer. I can explain to the police when they come, and—"

Irene rounded on him. Her eyes were large, warm and soft.

"That's what you think. I'm sick of hearing people say that you did it, because no one knows where you were for twenty-five minutes or so. I can't bear it no longer, and that's a fact. It's just plain silly, and I don't care what my mum or my dad says, either. There was nothing wrong in it, and I'm not ashamed."

She swung round, glaring in each direction in turn.

"I'm not in the *least* ashamed. Mr. Abel-Otty is a real nice man, and if his wife doesn't care for kissing that's her misfortune. Yes, I don't care if *she* hears, either! I suppose she's hiding somewhere, looking sour about her precious carpets. As though we haven't all lost carpets!

"Mr. Abel-Otty was with me—see? My mum was at the W.I. and the rest of the family was out. *I* was just going out, too, but I met him at the gate and he looked cold, so I said, 'Come in and get warm for a minute!' So he did, and very nice, too, and it's only because he's such a gentleman that he hasn't told everyone where he was before this. I told him it was silly not to, and I could stand it all right, specially as I'm going away.

"So you see, he couldn't have done the first murder and if he didn't do that one he wouldn't do the second, and he certainly couldn't have, anyhow, with a jug of cocoa in his hand, only people seem to have lost their wits; that's what I say. I don't know who did the murders—someone off their rocker, *if* you ask me—but it wasn't Mr. Abel-Otty and the whole lot of you can remember that and stop your hateful tongues wagging in *one* direction, at least, or they'll have me to reckon with." And she glared round aggressively, almost splendid in her great indignation.

"Oh, poor Mr. Abel-Otty!" murmured Emily to Caroline, who was still close by her side.

Mr. Abel-Otty, red to the ears and looking quite frantic, had been moving round her as though he were trying to tackle a difficult opponent. She had totally ignored his pleas for silence and his tortured expression.

"That's cooked his goose!" said Stephan compassionately. "He'd sooner be accused of murder than have his wife hear that."

"I can't see her, though."

"You can bet your boots she's here somewhere!"

"That's easy said, you shameless li'le 'ussy!" cried Mrs. Gotts, very loudly. " 'E put you up to it, I'd say. What better motive for murder than money, an' everyone knows 'is wife—"

Mr. Abel-Otty said loudly and furiously:

"If anyone else says a single word I shall have some people up for slander when we get in touch with the outside world again. All right, all right, Irene! I'm not angry with you, but I *told* you it wasn't necessary. Now see what you've done . . ." And he looked round, quite obviously searching for his wife's shocked and disapproving face.

The whole incident had had some of the elements of a play and the scene certainly had an arresting final curtain. As silence still lay over most of the church, and people's eyes were still fixed on the main actors in the drama, a figure came in briskly through the west door.

"Well!" said Mrs. Abel-Otty loudly, making her way towards Mrs. Pashley. "I've been down to have a look at the main road. It really isn't bad in places, except for the terrible mud. When I think of my carpets and furniture—"

A perceptible ripple went through the church and someone laughed rather hysterically. Mr. Abel-Otty swung round as though he had been stung and stared unbelievingly. Mrs. Abel-Otty, oblivious of the tension, chattered on in her self-centred way.

Emily felt that she could have flung herself down and roared with laughter. Mrs. Abel-Otty had not heard! Somehow, in her slightly light-headed state, that seemed absurdly funny. The chances were, too, that she never would hear, as she was so much less popular than her husband, even if, just then, some suspected him of murder.

Irene, with a baffled look, shrugged and walked away, moving her plump behind with dignity, and Mr. Abel-Otty, looking ready to collapse, sat down at the end of a pew. The tide of talk and small movements was resumed and the incident was over.

"All the same, it was really rather splendid of Irene!" said Caroline, smiling, and she went off to try to disentangle several small boys, who were fighting rather too realistically near the chancel steps.

Emily pulled herself together with an effort and realized that before the rescuers turned up again and began to assess conditions something would have to be done about the church. If the scene had been sordid yesterday it was a great deal worse today. She enlisted Mrs. Pashley, Mrs. Love and one or two of the more sensible women and, having sent as many of the children as possible out of doors, they set about trying to make order out of chaos. But it was very difficult. It was impossible yet to reach any of the houses, though it seemed likely that there would be hope of doing so within a very few hours, and the women, with nothing to do, were reluctant to be prized away from their whispering groups.

Emily, as she moved about the church, felt that she could do with an extra skin and ear-plugs. Her flesh literally shrank from the atmosphere that seemed to reach her from each group, and try as she would she could not fail to catch horrifying little snippets.

" 'Course it was the High girl! School-teachers aren't any

better than the rest an' she 'ad opportunity each time. Wait till the police come. We c'n tell 'em a thing or two—"

"I'd put my money on the Vicar, though 'e's always seemed so 'oly and kind. After all, you never c'n tell, an' it's bin known before that vicars—"

" 'Is missus looks right awful. Reckon she knows—and do she know *that*, poor woman—"

"I pity 'er if she thinks 'er 'usband—"

"Well, *I* don't. Think o' pore Mrs. Pike without a 'usband, an' that pore fatherless child—"

"Some father!" and a sniff.

"Well, 'e *was* 'er father. O' course Mrs. Long may 'ave done 'im in, but no one ac'ually saw '*er* in the churchyard, and she'd never throw a stone accurate enough. Takes practice, that. Now *I* favour the young chap. After all, 'e said—"

"The church will need fumigating for more reasons than one," Emily thought frantically. "Exorcizing, I should think."

She looked round for Betony, and, after a few moments, spied the child sitting huddled up on the stone seat in the south porch. She was writing in her diary and looked dirty and oddly shrunken. Mrs. Long was sitting a little apart, her hands plucking at her skirt and her eyes really wild.

"What *is* going to become of Betony?" Emily wondered. "I think I shall have to take her for a little; her mother's going to have a breakdown, that's obvious. This business has affected her direly. And all that led up to it, I suppose."

She came upon Stephan presently and poured out to him her pent-up uneasiness.

"If this doesn't end soon I shall get as queer-looking as Mrs. Long. I don't know *how* you manage to look so comparatively cheerful, and Caroline does, too. How can she, when she was alone in the churchyard at the time of the second murder and really is in a miserable position?"

Stephan stared.

"Alone in the churchyard last night? Caroline?"

"Well, she says she was. Someone saw her come in not long before—"

"But, my dear, sweet Aunt Emily, your precious Caroline was with *me*, and very nice, too, as Irene said. We were out there for half an hour or so, tucked cosily into the north porch out of the mist—"

A little of the weight rolled off Emily's heart.

"With *you?* Oh, Stephan, you *do* like her? Forgive me, but you mustn't just play with her, because . . ."

Stephan gave her an extremely quizzical look.

"Playing would do her a lot of good, as it happens. She's been too earnest for too long. Oh, yes, I *do* like her. I'm sorry I ever said she was cold and stiff. And I'm sorry she's had such a rotten time. She told me a bit about it; said she'd got round to telling you in the morning, and once started it looked as though she couldn't stop."

"And when you left her?"

"I went with her to the church door and shoved her in and then I was going down to get us both something to drink when I came in contact with that tombstone. I may have been a bit dazed and thoughtful; at all events it nearly laid me out at first. Mrs. Sainty and Dr. Love wouldn't hear of my going back to the church, so I sent her a message *and* some cocoa by Dr. Love—who is rather a sport, let me put on record. Hundreds may not believe us, but that's how it was and I'll stick to it till I'm on the steps of the scaffold."

"*Stephan!* I do wish you wouldn't make unsuitable jokes! They cut me to the heart just now."

"You ought to be jolly glad to hear any jokes at all. What's all that scuffle going on? Did I hear motor-horns? By Jove, I believe it's the rescuers!"

It was. To the wild excitement of the people of Marshton a fleet of lorries had managed to negotiate the main road to as far as the foot of the path down Church Hill. Everyone who could was soon swarming down the hill, and those who could not, like old Mrs. Gotts, sat waiting eagerly for news.

Had the police come, too? That was what Mrs. Gotts wanted to know, and she shook her head gloomily when told that they were following during the morning.

Emily paid little attention to the work of clearance that had already started down on the main road below. Once she went to the kissing-gate and gazed downwards at the strange, desolate scene, but there was much to do at the Vicarage, for Mrs. Sainty, seeing the end of the "siege" near at hand, was waxing anxious and rather fretful about the state of the place and the almost total absence of food and fuel.

By night, it was said, everyone would be accommodated in billets in two or three inland villages, and Mrs. Sainty was anxious to start restoring at any rate a measure of cleanliness to the Vicarage.

"Besides, there'll be the police," she said. "They'll need

somewhere to work."

"The police! They may be here any minute now!" Emily said aloud, when, after two hours' strenuous labour in the upper rooms, she went tiredly back to the church. She had scarcely seen Richard all morning. He was down in the mud-filled houses, doing what he could to rescue household possessions.

The mystery of the two murders weighed on her heart and all the time she had been working she had thought of nothing else. Over and over again she had visualized the churchyard on that momentous evening of wind and flood. First Richard, then Stephan, then perhaps Mrs. Long, Caroline, Betony. Where had Thomas Long come in the odd procession? If Mrs. Long had seen him ahead of her, then Stephan must have done so too. Unless, perhaps—and the possibility occurred to her for the first time—Thomas Long had somehow been *between* Stephan and Mrs. Long. But the track from the road to the kissing-gate was not really very long and it somehow seemed unlikely.

She found herself back amongst the piled furniture in the south aisle. The church was almost empty, except for Mrs. Gotts, who seemed to be dozing, with her head on a cushion. Suddenly a burst of brilliant sunshine flooded through the windows, sending faint blue patterns on to the creamy and rather chipped stone pillars.

Sunlight! It hardly seemed suitable, Emily thought, searching once more through the books. What *could* Mr. Pike have found that was so illuminating?

For five minutes she searched without result, then, thinking that she saw a book jammed between the desk and the next object, an armchair, she gave an impatient jerk at the desk. A large book fell with a thud from where it had been lodged, and with it fell another very small paper-backed book.

Emily knew what it was instantly, and instantly also the thing that had so maddeningly eluded her was clear. She picked up the little green book and stared at it blankly, while her heart went colder with pity and dread than it had done when the flood waters engulfed Marshton.

It might not mean what she thought it did—it might not! But, according to Peter, Mr. Pike had said, "There's only one person she would shield."

Chapter 15
THE BEST END, PERHAPS

EMILY stood there for a very long time, with the damp and stained little bus guide held against her chest. She could hear the somewhat stertorous breathing of Mrs. Gotts, shouts from below, and even, since the doors were open, the sound of a lark's song.

But she was conscious of nothing but the fact that she now had what was almost certainly a vital piece of knowledge. The thing that had never seemed quite right was now clear. But did it really mean that there had been a witness of the murder? A witness who should never, certainly, have seen such a sight?

The murderer must have seen Mr. Pike's mind working as he looked at the local bus guide, and the fact that he had died so soon afterwards could only mean that his new knowledge was important.

"I don't want to be murdered myself before I can pass it on," she thought, looking round warily. "I wonder why the murderer didn't remove the book? Couldn't find it, perhaps, as it was so well jammed between the desk and the chair."

She moved uneasily away. Evil had certainly followed Mr. Pike very quickly, and if she, too, had been seen understanding the significance of the little green book she might not be any too safe. But there was one person who, all along, had been in mortal danger.

"First of all I shall have to tackle her. I shall have to find out what she *did* see. All along I thought she was more upset than perhaps she should have been."

She was leaving by way of the south porch when she spied a second small book, this time on the stone floor, almost hidden by the base of an ancient cross that had once stood in the churchyard. It was Betony's diary. Evidently the child had dropped it and it had perhaps got kicked out of the way during the stampede to the bottom of the hill.

Emily picked up the book and stared almost unseeingly down at the round childish writing. Betony's diary, of all things to find at that moment! And she saw in her mind's eye the child's pale head bent over the small pages as she wrote and wrote. What had Betony been writing during those many hours of boredom and fear? How, above all, was it that the child was still safe? Unless perhaps the murderer didn't suspect . . .

Yes, she would have to find out the exact truth immediately, not only because the murderer would have to be brought to justice, but because it would save a number of secrets from being revealed to the painful light of day. If the truth were known there would be no need for the police to enquire into things that might, at one time, have seemed relevant.

As she went down the hill the lark sang louder than ever, a lovely, throbbing song, and the scene below was very strange. The walls and fences were festooned with curtains, carpets and bed-linen, all grey-green with mud and slime. Children were screaming as they dashed in and out of the houses, carrying what they could. There was mud up to their thighs. Dogs barked and gambolled.

The tension seemed to have gone from everyone except Emily herself. With all her heart she hated what she had to do, because she knew she could hardly bear to see more fear and sorrow on a little pale face.

She came to the bottom of the lane at last, where the mud was still deep and slippery, and her gaze searched the crowd for whom she sought.

People were much too interested in what was going on to take any notice of her. There were lorries and Army trucks stretching for some distance up the road and even a car or two, very muddy indeed. A little to the left a young constable was refusing entry to some anxious people in a shabby Ford, who wanted to try to get to one of the farms to see how their relatives had fared.

So there were police of some kind. But not the kind to deal with murder, Emily rightly assumed, wondering how long the detectives would be.

Outside his house Emily could see Dr. Love and she began to walk carefully in his direction, looking about her all the time. Only the crown of the road was comparatively clear, and even so it was crossed in places with water a foot or two deep. The sun was hot on her head and she seemed to have no energy at all.

Just as she neared Dr. Love's house one of the last lorries in the line sprang into life and Emily saw it back violently, so that a cloud of filthy water was thrown into the air. Then quickly it spun round, slithering on the bad surface, and in another few moments was driving away inland. Another constable appeared suddenly in the road, but he was too late to stop the vehicle and he was left staring blankly after it.

It was as the lorry turned that Emily had a glimpse into the cab, and with a smothered cry she quickened her pace. A few moments later someone cried shrilly:

"Dr. Love! Dr. Love! Did you see who it was took the lorry? She's made a bolt for it with the child!"

Dr. Love had spun round and was staring after the lorry as it lurched and bumped and skidded along the road, and Emily arrived breathlessly at his side.

"I was just too late! I was coming to find them—Betony! I *had* to talk to her! She saw the murder, I'm nearly certain, and now—oh, we must go after them! We must save the child!"

Dr. Love's face was grave and he acted quickly. There was a car nearby—a muddy Austin belonging to relations of the Loves, who had come to see what they could do—and the ignition key was there. The doctor said briefly:

"Come on! The woman must be crazy! You mean she did it and the kid saw? That poor little devil!"

Emily, almost wordless, climbed in beside him, and he backed the car with some difficulty.

"We'll have trouble with that constable. Got orders to see that no one leaves. Now look here, officer! You can come with us, if you like, but don't try and stop us. I'm a doctor, and that poor woman who's got away with the lorry is as mad as a hatter. It doesn't matter so much what happens to her, but we've got to save the child!"

The constable hesitated, quite obviously not liking his bewildering task at all, and Dr. Love drove away with scant ceremony.

"We'll be locked up later, perhaps. Who cares? Got to keep them in sight!"

"I didn't know she could drive!" Emily gasped.

"Oh, yes. She used to help her husband with the taxi service when he had it. Gave it up just before your time. But she certainly isn't used to that type of heavy lorry and the road's appalling. I heard just now that there are some shockingly bad places still, where the land drops. The man who owns this car—my brother-in-law, as a matter of fact—said he only just managed to get it through."

They were not very far behind the lorry, which was not travelling fast, though occasionally it forged ahead for a short distance. Whenever the speed was increased it skidded dangerously, and once it swung a trifle up a low bank.

Emily sat tensely, with clasped hands, no longer knowing what to think or what to hope.

"Would it be kinder, after all, to let them go? They'll be sent back, anyway. They couldn't get right away."

"I think we ought to get that child out of her mother's hands at once," Dr. Love said grimly. "There's hope for the kid, even after all she's gone through, but none for the mother. She must have gone pretty well raving. I've hated the look of her, and I gave her a mild sedative last night, but there was not much I could do. Of course I didn't fully understand; I just thought it was her husband's treatment and sudden death that had unhinged her. We can't leave the child in her hands in case she thinks *she's* better dead."

"I know. That's what I'm afraid of." And Emily sat in silence again as the car managed fairly steadily to follow the lorry's progress. Occasionally Dr. Love sounded the horn, trying to convey a signal to the woman at the wheel ahead, but Mrs. Long ignored it or did not hear.

Dimly Emily was conscious of the strange beauty of the partly flooded fields, with the blue sky reflected in the water and the heights of Blane Beacon very clear in the distance. Further inland there were other slight uplands, bright brown where the plough had passed. Uplands that would later, in an unimaginable summer, blaze with the silver-gold of barley.

The lorry ahead was travelling faster now, though, if anything, the road was worse. Dr. Love swore under his breath, but he would not risk his own passenger by putting on a speed that might be dangerous.

"What is she hoping to do? What can she hope to gain? Even if we lose them she'll be caught and brought back."

"I'm terribly afraid—she isn't sane!" said Emily. "She may think it necessary—oh, drive faster!"

"Not on your life! I don't know this car and the road's appalling here. I had no idea the flood waters had managed to get so far inland. Look! She's nearing the low bridge! Oh, my God!" And Dr. Love braked so suddenly that the car skidded wildly for a moment, but came to a safe resting-place at the side of the road, near the point where the narrow little bridge made a dangerous curve.

"Oh! Oh!" Emily had had eyes only for the scene ahead. The accident—if accident it was—was over in a split second. Mrs. Long had driven the lorry straight off the road instead of taking the bridge. The big vehicle went crashing on its side in what was still several feet of water in a deep hollow, and utter silence descended on the scene.

Sick and shivering Emily opened the car door.

"We'll have to go and see. There may be something we can do."

"There may," said the doctor grimly and got out on his own side, slipping on the bad surface of the road.

There had always been a river flowing through deep hollows at that point and now, in the fields on either side, the flood waters still lay outspread, faintly stirred by the extending ripples that were all that remained, already, of the violence of the crash.

The lorry poked up at an angle out of the water, but the cabin was low, almost submerged. Emily would have scrambled frantically towards it, but Dr. Love héld her back.

"You stay here and signal for help if any more lorries come past. I'll do what I can, but it's almost sure to be too late."

"She's done what she intended," said Emily.

The doctor, with immense care, at last managed to work his way along the side of the lorry until the driver's window was immediately below him. She saw him crouch down and seize something. A second later a wet red hand and wrist came into view.

" 'Fraid she's dead!" the doctor called back after a moment. "Must have hit her head. There's a great cut. The child's underneath her; not moving. Probably dead, too—drowned. Impossible to get them out until we can fetch ropes and tackle."

"Oh, are you quite sure?" Emily remembered Betony

saying: "It must be a nightmare! Shall we wake up, Mrs. Varney?" And now she would never wake up again. It might be for the best—she might one day realize that it was definitely so—but just then she would have given much to speak to the child, to comfort her and tell her that life might still be lived happily and peacefully.

"Quite sure. She's deep under water and the chances are that she never even struggled. She could easily have hit her head as well as they went over."

Dr. Love, not without getting himself very wet, retraced his way to her side and just at that moment a car came along, travelling slowly towards Marshton. Emily noticed the word "Police" as the car stopped and a grave-faced, middle-aged man spoke quickly.

"Has there been an accident?"

"Yes, I'm afraid so," said Dr. Love, equally briskly. "I'm a doctor, but there's nothing I can do. Both dead. We think it closes the murder case, but now, I suppose, there'll never be any real evidence—"

"I'm Detective-Inspector Yarwood of Norwich, and this is Sergeant Lines. We should have been here before, but we skidded and had a bad puncture not far up the road. We heard there'd been a murder—"

"Two murders," said Emily faintly. "And I think there may be evidence. I believe I have it with me. But thank God there's someone to take over." And she would have slipped down on to the muddy road if the doctor had not seized her and held her until the dizziness passed.

Chapter 16
EMILY PRODUCES THE EVIDENCE

BY THE time that dusk fell that night the inhabitants of Marshton were variously disposed of amongst friends and strangers inland, the houses that stood furthest away from the marsh had been cleared of the worst of the mud, and furniture and carpets were drying in every slightly raised field.

With the official announcement that the name of the murderer was known and the case in hand the worst of the tension had relaxed, and somehow the truth had got about, no one quite knew how. Part of it was truth that no one wanted to hear, but, as Mrs. Pashley said:

"It's better to know. The uncertainty just couldn't have gone on."

Marshton, as the dusk fell, made a strange sight, infinitely desolate and derelict, and yet there was no one who doubted that the damaged houses would be rebuilt, the Blane Bank reinforced and that the village would one day be itself again; if not soon, then as soon as willing hands and the available money could make it. Much the same thing had been achieved in other places on the Norfolk coast and sturdy villages do not die easily.

The church was dim and deserted; the stoves and lamps were out and the windows had all been opened to let out the varied smells that had gathered during the days and nights of flood. The furniture was still there, and there would certainly be more added to it, for there was really nowhere else where it could go.

Down the lane at the Vicarage, after a somewhat makeshift but peaceful tea, a number of people gathered round a log-fire in the sitting-room. There was still no electricity, and, as darkness fell, Emily lit a couple of lamps and scattered candles here and there. Richard sat tiredly in his favourite chair near the fire, Stephan perched on a small but solid table in a corner, and Caroline High had the chair next to Emily. Mr. Abel-Otty was there, though he was shortly to join his wife at an inland hotel, and Colonel Pashley and Dr. Love. Detective-Inspector Yarwood and the sergeant completed the party.

The story of the past two days and nights had been told and many people questioned, and it was now fairly clear what had happened. To Emily's relief much that was now irrelevant had been left unsaid. People would forget in time that Mr. Abel-Otty had enjoyed himself with Irene Woodrow, that Stephan had threatened to kill Thomas Long, and that both the Vicar and his wife were said to have secrets. The villagers might wonder for a little while, but the police, apparently, would not care, and something, at the last, seemed to have tied the wagging tongues. They were not bad people, after all, Emily supposed.

"What I don't see is," Mr. Abel-Otty remarked rather testily, "how Emily here knew that the child had witnessed the murder and was so sure that it was the mother."

"I didn't *know*," Emily Varney said. "That is to say, I had no real evidence. I always thought that Betony knew a bit more than she would admit, and then, when I saw the bus time-table, I realized what had been nagging me all the time. After all, the murder could have been done *before* six o'clock, but we got confused by all the people passing through the churchyard. Actually, I can't imagine now why we never asked ourselves what Thomas Long was doing after he left the inn at about twenty to six, since it couldn't have taken him much longer than ten minutes to get up to the churchyard, even if he was fairly drunk. And if it *had* been done before six o'clock then Betony could easily have been a witness. Going on from that it was clear to me at once that there was only one person she would protect to that extent."

"Her mother was always one of the chief suspects, wasn't she?" Detective-Inspector Yarwood asked mildly. "But she wasn't seen to go near the churchyard until she went up the track at ten past six, when, if her husband had been anywhere in front of her, he would almost certainly have been seen by Mr. Stephan Varney. The murder, it was thought, had not been committed until after six o'clock and Mrs. Long was seen down at the pub about then." He glanced down at Mr. Pike's plan, which the Colonel had thought fit to give him, though much of the other 'evidence' had been suppressed. "Good God! There does seem to have been a devil of a lot of coming and going through that churchyard on a bad night! But it would be better for Mrs. Varney to tell you how she began to see the case clearly."

"I'm afraid it was a very easy case really, and you would have seen the solution almost at once if you'd been here," Emily said slowly. "It was just that we were all too close to it, and the child was in such a nervous state that we didn't want to bother her any more than we could help. I knew all the time that there was something we'd missed.

"Betony, when she came to me at twenty to seven, told me that she had stayed late at school. She got off the bus just past her own gate and then couldn't face going home. So she turned up the lane to the churchyard and came to borrow a book from here. I *had* lent her quite a number. I just never thought about the bus at the time, because I was already worried to think of my husband out in that awful wind with a bad cold. And I never thought of it later, when Mr. Pike was questioning people. Again she told him that she got off the bus and came straight up to the Vicarage, but while she was talking she felt sick and had to dash out of the room. We all felt terrible—even Mr. Pike, I think. It seemed almost as though we had been bullying her, though really, of course, we hadn't at all.

"Later she confessed that she had seen the body and been frightened and she seemed to be suffering from guilt because she hadn't got help immediately. That seemed fully to account, at the time, for her very tense and unsettled behaviour.

"Later still, Mr. Pike must have picked up the little green bus guide from amongst those books rescued from the flood, and, probably looking at it idly, saw that there was only one bus that Betony *could* have come on. That's the one that should get round to the shop at ten to six, and it would be a minute or two earlier when Betony got off at her own gate. The next bus isn't due till six-forty-five—the one that Mrs. Sainty came on just before the flood—and then there's only one more, except on Saturdays.

"The minute I looked at the bus guide I realized how slow we'd been, because there was all that time to account for. So I began to see, though of course it was still only surmise, that she must have turned up to the track to the churchyard and seen her father some way ahead, with her mother behind him. Perhaps Mrs. Long had followed him because he looked so very drunk, or perhaps she knew all along what she was going to do.

"Anyway, it turns out that I was right, for it's all in Betony's diary. She saw them in front of her and followed slowly, not wanting to be seen. She watched her father cross the churchyard and turn towards the south porch and she saw her mother suddenly throw the stone that killed him. Her mother apparently never saw Betony at all, and, after bending over the body, she went swiftly back down the hill. That was when she went to the pub to enquire for her husband, hoping and trusting, of course, that on such a night no one would have noticed her following him. Later, when Mrs. Herring saw her, she must have had a half-formed resolve to go back to the churchyard and make absolutely sure that he was dead.

"As for poor Betony, she adored her mother and hated her father, but it must have been an impossible thing to swallow—that her mother had committed murder. As for Mr. Pike, Mrs. Long had guessed that Betony must have got off that bus and had seen what had happened, and she'd know that the moment everyone realized there was all that time unaccounted for they would start thinking on quite different lines. So she decided that Mr. Pike must die before he could tell anyone. It's a wonder she didn't play safer still and kill the child, but she was fond of Betony and perhaps she wasn't quite crazy enough for that."

"I suppose there's no evidence that Mrs. Long did the second murder?" said Stephan.

"Yes, there is. The police found a blood-stained mackintosh in the field by the lane, and a few threads of her blue skirt caught on the churchyard wall. She must have come back without a coat, but no one noticed." And Emily looked at Detective-Inspector Yarwood, who nodded.

"Yes, she did it all right, but people weren't in the mood to be observant, evidently. You know, having read that diary, it seems to me as well that that little girl didn't live to face the future. Such a sensitive child could never have lived with all that terrible knowledge."

"She *was* very sensitive," said Emily, with a quiver in her voice. "She loved all beauty; particularly the beauty of words." She held Betony's diary in her hands. "I—I know you'll want to take it away, but first could I—could I read them a little of it? I think they ought to know—to realize what she went through."

"Yes, read it," said the middle-aged stranger. "It's a very sad and illuminating document."

"To think that she was writing it almost every time I looked at her!" said Emily, turning the pages slowly. "And to think that her mother didn't realize just what she was doing! There's a very short entry written in school on Tuesday morning. That was the day of the flood. She writes: 'I've got five minutes while I'm having my milk and biscuits. Don't feel I want to talk to anyone. They're all nattering about what a beast Miss Sharp is because she's given them extra homework. It doesn't seem to matter. Nothing matters a bit today. My head aches and things keep on going round and round in my head like those goldfish in the pet-shop window. Round and round. I simply dread the thought of going home, but I've got to. I can't run away to work on the land or anything like that because of mother, who has only me. Anyway, I'm not old enough.

" 'I hate, hate, hate my father for the way he treated mother last night. He was awful to me, but I could bear that. It's when he bullies and hits mother that I could kill him. She used to be pretty and now she isn't a bit any more, just white and whispy, with horrid red hands, and such a queer look sometimes.

" 'Sometimes I wonder if life's worth while, though the Head often says in her speeches about being a good citizen and living for others. Sometimes I'd like to live just for me, in a lovely little cottage far out on the marshes. I might call it Sea Lavender Cottage and I'd keep a dog and a cat and watch the sky over the marsh all day, so big and high and bright. Break is over. Gosh! I nearly spilled my milk and if anyone else shouts at me I shall howl like a silly kid and then that beast Edith Mackerel will jeer. It's English, anyway. I like that'."

The shadowy room was very still. Stephan moved quietly over to Caroline and sat on the arm of her chair, and Emily was glad, for she saw that Caroline was very much moved. Mr. Abel-Otty puffed moodily at his pipe—now replenished—and the Colonel cleared his throat.

"The next entry," said Emily, "was written in the church after the flood. She says: 'I keep on reading and reading Yeats' lovely poems, kind of trying to fill my mind with them. But it doesn't really work. I wish I could be on Innisfree, with nine bean rows and a hive and all the rest of the lovely things. And I don't care a bit that it's really Cat Island. Mrs. Varney says she thinks it is.

" 'Some of the poems I almost have to forget. *The wind blows out of the gates of the day, The wind blows over the lonely of heart, And the lonely of heart are withered away* frightens me tonight. I feel as though I am being withered and as though no one on earth can stop it happening to me. Because I have seen the supremely awful thing. I have seen my mother—my own mother—do what I have sometimes thought in my wickedest moments that I should like to do. She committed murder. She was there in front of me as I started up towards the churchyard, and *he* was there further in front still and very drunk. And when I got to the gate I peeped over to see what they were doing, because I was so much afraid of my father and even my mother's back looked queer. And I saw her throw the stone. I didn't know she could throw like that. I hid, and she went away, after just looking down at him. So then I had to *make* myself go and look at him and I was certain he was dead. I thought at first I ought to get someone, but I couldn't, and I went away and was sick in a corner of the churchyard, where there's that awful marble vault with a sort of half-blocked entrance. And I crouched down there while it got darker, and I told myself that I was still Betony Long, but it didn't work, perhaps because I didn't really want to be. I could only remember that my mother was a murderess, and I wished I was dead, too, though I wonder if there really is a hell.

" 'I longed to go in the church and ask God to forgive mother. That was where I meant to go first, when I got off the bus. It seemed the only thing to do after a perfectly awful day, for it's so beautiful it always helps. In the end I knew I couldn't go near my father again and I went to the Vicarage and Mrs. Varney was kind. I don't know what I should do without her. She stops me feeling lonely of heart'." Emily's voice shook, though she steadied it almost immediately.

"There's a lot more about what it was like in the church and how much the flood frightened her. Then about lunch-time yesterday she goes on: 'Writing in my diary makes me feel better. My precious, secret little book! How scared I always was that father would get it. Oh, I feel so awful. I don't know now what I'm thinking or saying, and I've told lies to Mrs. Varney. And yet some of it was true. I *did* see my father and I did wonder if I ought to tell someone he was there. I *have* to tell lies, really, because if people know you've done murder they hang you by the neck until you are dead, and I can't bear that to happen to my own mother.

" 'Why can't things unhappen? I'm frightened, too, because the village people think a lot of other people did it. I want to bite and scratch them because they're such idiots. I think mother's beginning to guess that I saw. She asked what bus I came on and I just couldn't speak. Mother's an awful witch; it's just no good trying to keep things from her, and she looks at me so queerly that I feel sick all the time.'

"She goes on and on," said Emily, her voice harsh with pain and weariness and her eyes very large and dark. "It's all here, almost to the moment when her mother made her hurry down to the lorries. She was writing in the south porch. Poor Betony! I do think now that it's as well her mother took her with her."

"I wonder if any of us will ever be happy again?" said Caroline sombrely, and Stephan said quickly:

"Of course we will. The flood came and brought a jolly lot of things we didn't like, but the water's going down and some day it will all be forgotten."

"Quite right," said Richard Varney. "The next task is to try to get the village back to normal in as short a time as possible. Though I'm afraid it will be a good while before the houses on the marsh road are habitable. And now what about more logs for the fire, and coffee for some of you people before you go over those awful roads? We've talked for a long time."

"I'm glad, though, that we heard Betony's diary," said Caroline. "It somehow makes her death easier to bear."

Emily nodded.

"She didn't know that she was leaving it for us. Yes, I'm glad, too, in a strange way, though I think I shall never read a sadder document."

It was the end of July and the weather was hot and brilliant, but Marshton Church was cool and shadowy, except where the sunlight poured through the pale blue and white windows in the south aisle. The church was white and still and almost as it had looked before the flood, but, even though some months had passed, there were still two bulging armchairs, a table and various odds and ends that no one had ever claimed.

"Soon they'll have to go. They can't stay here as a sort of memorial of those days," thought Emily Varney fleetingly. She was kneeling at one side of the chancel steps, giving a final tweak here and there to the wild flowers in a huge pottery vase. She had already done the altar flowers and the ones in the side chapels and these were the last and most lovely: poppies, corn-marigolds, scabious, toadflax and long trailing tendrils of vetch.

She stood up slowly and surveyed them with infinite satisfaction. Surely there had never been such a year for wild flowers? It was almost as though the land were intending to make up for the miseries of the spring. The corn-marigolds made acres and acres of barley and oats glow with an almost incredible blaze of yellow, poppies flared silky and scarlet everywhere, interwoven with the purity of white campion and marguerites. The huge, pale jar seemed to hold the very essence of summer, gathered by herself and Richard on the previous evening as they walked slowly through the fields.

Emily was certainly pregnant; she expected her baby in October. But she was very well and was still able to walk quite long distances. After the strain and bitterness of those days of flood and tragedy she had felt very unwell for a time, but now her natural splendid health had returned and she was happier than she had ever been.

It was possible now, she thought, walking slowly backwards up the central aisle to assess the glowing beauty of her flower arrangements, to see the results of the flood, and they were not all of them bad. In fact, disaster and death had left in their train some things that were very good. Herself and Richard, for instance, now in complete accord, and Caroline and Stephan. That looked as though it were going to be the most worth-while thing of all. Mr. Abel-Otty had finished his book now, even though he had lost all his notes, and he and his wife had just moved back to their house on the edge of the marsh. Mrs. Abel-Otty never seemed to have heard the gossip about her husband's amorous adventures, or if she had she had decided to ignore the information.

"Wise woman!" thought Emily. For, after all, Mrs. Abel-Otty enjoyed being the wife of quite a well-known Norfolk writer and lecturer, and why should she throw away a perfectly good husband because he was over-fond of the kisses she had no wish to give?

Stephan had been back in London for some months, and his eye really seemed as though it was going to be all right, but just then he was staying at the Vicarage for his summer fortnight. Emily thought that he had altered; he was gentler and less cynical and he seemed very happy. Caroline High had a good job in a London school and they had been meeting regularly all summer. They were, in fact, likely to announce their engagement at any time; Emily suspected that Stephan already had the ring and that the moment he saw Caroline again . . .

Quietly she crossed to the plain windows of the north

aisle. She leaned her arms on a stone sill and gazed down at the peaceful summer scene. There were the little red-roofed houses, the bright boats, the spreading marsh and the sea very blue beyond the Blane Bank. Only the fact that there were still cranes on the bank, and that she knew that men were working furiously during the calm weather, reminded her of the flood. But of course she knew, too, that many of the little houses on the marsh road were still uninhabited. As in so many other places along the coast, new houses were going up further inland, though at Marshton almost the only rising ground was on Church Hill.

Emily leaned and stared and felt thankful that she had not persuaded Richard to apply for a living elsewhere. At first it had seemed impossible to settle down again amongst the people with whom they had shared the horror, and by whom they had been so suspiciously regarded. But the feeling had passed. Once people had known the identity of the murderer the suspicions had died, or at least they had been buried very deeply.

Friendliness had soon come back to Marshton, as the people themselves drifted back to their houses from the villages inland. The shop was rebuilt now, but Mrs. Grief and Minnie no longer presided behind the counter, to the relief of many, including Emily herself. She had never liked or trusted either of them and if they had stayed she would almost certainly have insisted on leaving. But Mrs. Grief had gone to live with a married daughter near King's Lynn and Minnie was serving in the grocery department of a big store in Norwich. It was said that she was being courted by the assistant manager, a widower with a fifteen-year-old son, but that Emily was slow to believe, though she would have been glad to know that Minnie had a chance of happiness.

Emily herself had been working hard on a new book all summer. The one that she had been correcting on that momentous March evening had been published in June and her Press cuttings were even more enthusiastic than usual. It really seemed that A. E. Sebastian could not go wrong. But her identity was still a secret from the villagers of Marshton, though she sometimes thought it might be as well to let it become general knowledge. She had grown to hate unnecessary secrets.

The Longs were almost never mentioned in Marshton now, but Emily thought sometimes of Betony and it was she who, at dusk, put sea lavender on her grave. Sentimental and unnecessary, she had told herself, but Betony had loved it so and it would remind Emily of the child for ever.

There was plenty of work waiting for her down at the Vicarage, and she certainly should not linger, dreaming, at the window. But as she swung round, fully awake at last, there were footsteps in the north porch and the heavy old door opened noisily. Emily had not even noticed anyone walking across the churchyard.

It was Stephan, very sun-tanned and healthy-looking. But he had put on weight during his enforced inactivity, a fact that worried him more than a little. Behind him was Caroline, wearing a yellow frock and with her red hair shining. Her eyes, too, had a light in them, and, as she came forward smiling, Emily caught the gleam of a ring.

"Well, here she is!" said Stephan. "The train was bang on time, and I drove back here like a shot from a gun. By Jove, as the Colonel would say, that new car of yours can travel, Aunt Emily."

"I know it can, but it doesn't often get the chance," remarked Emily, and kissed Caroline warmly.

"My dear, how well you look and how—" She was going to say "how beautiful", but Stephan got in first.

"Yes, I've been telling her she's exquisite all the way from Norwich and she's just about beginning to believe me."

Caroline laughed, though she looked shy.

"I do—almost. It's a lovely feeling. But it does seem queer to be back here! How gay and bright everywhere looks in this sunshine. I made Stephan stop so that I could pick some flowers. I see that you've been doing the same."

"Yes," said Emily. "I can't resist Norfolk in high summer. And now come down to the Vicarage and have lunch."

"And you'll tell me all the news?"

"All the news," Emily promised, and led the way from the church. "But first we must drink to that new ring and to your future happiness."

Also published by
Greyladies

DEATH ON TIPTOE
by R. C. Ashby
(Ruby Ferguson)

In *Death on Tiptoe,* originally published in 1931, the classic ingredients of the traditional country houseparty whodunnit are transformed into a deliciously different Gothic murder mystery with literary allusions galore.

Against the backdrop of the crumbling Cleys Castle on the Welsh Border Marches, lowering with centuries of dark brooding menace, the houseparty guests dress up in ancient Tudor costumes and play hide-and-seek - in the dark. It should come as no surprise when this leads to trouble. Gradually the veneer of upper-class well-mannered sophistication disintegrates, exposing dark secrets, greed and ruthless ambition.

Keep the lights on.

MURDER WHILE YOU WORK
by Susan Scarlett
(Noel Streatfeild)

Noel Streatfeild used her own experience of munitions factory work, Civil Defence and the W.V.S. in World War II for the setting of this her only murder mystery. The background detail is superb, from letting the capstan turret swing in time to 'Coming Home on a Wing and a Prayer' to looking forward (?) to fried spam for tea.

Judy Rest, the newest recruit to the factory, has an odd billet in the village but refuses to move despite unsettling deaths in the house. In an atmosphere of increasing gothic creepiness, Judy and Nick, a brilliant young explosives researcher, work out not by whom, for that's pretty obvious, but why and how the family, including the dog, are being murdered one by one. Add to this a portrait of a disturbed child, at which Miss Streatfeild excels, a nicely forthright Lady and, of course, a spot of restrained romance, for a real treat from a well-loved author.